"Filled with a lush, explicit er[illegible] nd sly punning that stret[illegible] l."

—[illegible]irkus

D0591504

"About as fu[illegible] . He has a dozen ways o[illegible] you laugh. . . . One of the most entertaining novels I have read in a long time."

—Granville Hicks,
The American Way

"A cross between Bellow's Herzog and Nabokov's Humbert. . . ."

—*New York Times Book Review*

"Outrageous and outstanding. . . . Beautiful work."

—*The National Observer*

"A flawless and utterly compelling work. His wit, intelligent sympathy, and unequaled command of the potentialities of the language for expressing and revealing have never had a better union. . . . One of Updike's finest achievements."

—*The Charlotte Observer*

Fawcett Crest and Premier Books
by John Updike:

THE POORHOUSE FAIR, *a novel*
THE SAME DOOR, *short stories*
RABBIT, RUN, *a novel*
PIGEON FEATHERS *and other stories*
THE CENTAUR, *a novel*
VERSE, *poems*
ASSORTED PROSE
OF THE FARM, *a novel*
THE MUSIC SCHOOL, *short stories*
COUPLES, *a novel*
MIDPOINT *and other poems*
BECH: A BOOK
RABBIT REDUX, *a novel*
MUSEUMS AND WOMEN *and other stories*
A MONTH OF SUNDAYS, *a novel*

ARE THERE FAWCETT PAPERBACKS
YOU WANT BUT CANNOT FIND IN YOUR LOCAL STORES?

You can get any title in print in Fawcett Crest, Fawcett Premier, or Fawcett Gold Medal editions. Simply send title and retail price, plus 35¢ to cover mailing and handling costs for each book wanted, to:

MAIL ORDER DEPARTMENT,
FAWCETT PUBLICATIONS,
P.O. Box 1014
GREENWICH, CONN. 06830

Books are available at discounts in quantity lots for industrial or sales-promotional use. For details write FAWCETT WORLD LIBRARY, CIRCULATION MANAGER, FAWCETT BLDG., GREENWICH, CONN. 06830

John Updike

A MONTH OF SUNDAYS

A FAWCETT CREST BOOK

Fawcett Publications, Inc., Greenwich, Connecticut

A MONTH OF SUNDAYS

THIS BOOK CONTAINS THE COMPLETE TEXT OF THE ORIGINAL HARDCOVER EDITION.

A Fawcett Crest Book reprinted by arrangement with Alfred A. Knopf, Inc.

Copyright © 1974, 1975 by John Updike

All rights reserved, including the right to reproduce this book or portions thereof in any form.

All the characters in this book are fictitious, and any resemblance to actual persons living or dead is purely coincidental.

An excerpt from this book originally appeared in *Playboy* magazine.

Alternate Selection of the Book-of-the-Month Club, February 1975.

Printed in the United States of America

First printing: February 1976

1 2 3 4 5 6 7 8 9 10

for Judith Jones

---

my tongue is the pen of a ready writer

—PSALM 45

This principle of soul, universally and individually, is the principle of ambiguity.

—PAUL TILLICH

1

Forgive me my denomination and my town; I am a Christian minister, and an American. I write these pages at some point in the time of Richard Nixon's unravelling. Though the yielding is mine, the temptation belongs to others: my keepers have set before me a sheaf of blank sheets—a month's worth, in their estimation. Sullying them is to be my sole therapy.

My bishop, bless his miter, has ordered (or, rather, offered as the alternative to the frolicsome rite of defrocking) me brought here to the desert, far from the green and crowded land where my parish, as the French so nicely put it, locates itself. The month is to be one of recuperation—as I think of it, "retraction," my condition being officially diagnosed as one of "distraction." Perhaps the opposite of "dis" is not "re" but the absence of any prefix, by which construal I am spiritual brother to those broken-boned athletes who must spend a blank month, amid white dunes and midnight dosages, in "traction." I doubt (verily, my name *is* Thomas) it will work. In *my* diagnosis I suffer from nothing less virulent than the human condition, and so would preach it. Though the malady is magnificent, I should in honest modesty add that my own case is scarcely feverish, and pustular only if we cross-examine the bed linen. Masturbation! Thou saving grace-note upon the baffled chord of self! Paeans to St. Onan, later.

I feel myself warming to this, which is not my intent. Let my distraction remain intractable. No old prestidigitator amid the tilted mirrors of sympathetic counselling will let himself be pulled squeaking from this glossy, last-resort, false-bottomed topper.

Particulars!* The motel—I resist calling it a sanatorium, or halfway house, or detention center—has the shape of an O, or, more exactly, an omega. The ring of rooms encircling the pool is fronted by two straight corridors, containing to the left the reception desk, offices, rest rooms sexually distinguished by bovine silhouettes, and a tiny commissary heavy on plastic beadwork and postcards of dinosaur bones but devoid of any magazines or journals that might overexcite the patients—oops, the guests—with topical realities. The other way, along the other foot of the Ω, lie the restaurant and bar.

* As Allen Ginsberg intones in one of the cantos of the new Bible waiting for the winds to unscatter it.

The glass wall of the bar is tinted a chemical purple through which filters a desert vista of diminishing sagebrush and distant, pale, fossiliferous mountains. The restaurant wall, at least at breakfast, wears heavy vanilla curtains out of whose gaps knives of light fall upon the grapefruit and glass of the set tables with an almost audible splintering of brightness. The place seems, if not deserted, less than half full. All middle-aged men, we sit each at our table clearing dry throughts* and suppressing nervous gossip among the silverware. I feel we are a "batch," more or less recently arrived. We are pale. We are stolid. We are dazed. The staff, who peek and move about as if preparatory to an ambush, appear part twanging, leathery Caucasians, their blue eyes bleached to match the alkaline sky and the seat of their jeans, and the rest nubile aborigines whose silent tread and stiff black hair uneasily consort with the frilled pistachio uniforms the waitresses perforce wear. I felt, being served this morning, dealt with reverentially, or dreadfully, as if in avoidance of contamination. A potential topic: touch and the sacred. God as Supreme Disease. *Noli me tangere.* Germs and the altar. The shared chalice versus the disposable paper cuplet: how many hours of my professional life have been chewed to bitter shreds (the apocalyptic antisepticist among the deacons

* Meant to type "throats," was thinking "thoughts," a happy Freudian, let it stand. The typewriter, which they have provided me after I assured them I was a man of my time, no penman, is new, and races ahead of my fingertips ofttimes. The air is quick.

versus the holisticer-than-thou holdouts for the big Grail) by this liturgical debate. Never mind. I am free of that, for a month or forever. Good criddence.*

What can I tell you? I arrived at midnight, disoriented. The airport hellishly clean, a fine dry wind blowing. Little green bus manned by pseudo-cowpoke took us into an enormous hour of swallowing desert dark. Met at the glass doors by a large lady, undeformed but unattractive, no doubt chosen for that very quality in this sensitive post. Seemed to be manageress. Named, if my ears, still plugged with jet-hum, deceived me not, Ms. Prynne. Face of a large, white, inexplicably self-congratulating turtle. White neck extended as if to preen or ease a chafing. Snapped rules at us. Us: beefy Irish priest and a third initiate, a slurring shy Tennesseean, little hunched man with the hopeful quick smile of a backslider, probably some derelict revivalist who doubled as a duping insurance agent. Rules (as passed on to our hostess by the sponsoring bishoprics and conference boards): meals at eight, twelve-thirty, and seven. Bar open from noon. Commissary closed between two and five. Mornings: write, *ad libidum*. Afternoons: physical exercise, preferably golf, though riding, swimming, tennis facilities do exist. Evenings: board or card games, preferably poker. Many no-nos. No serious discus-

* Intentional this time: riddance applied to credence.

sions, doctrinal or intrapersonal. No reading except escapist: a stock of English detective and humorous fiction from between the two world wars available in the commissary lending library. The Bible above all is banned. No religion, no visitors, no letters in or out. No trips to town (nearest town 40 m. off, named Sandstone) though some field trips would be bussed later in the month.

But you know all this. Who are you, gentle reader?

Who am I?

I go to the mirror. The room still nudges me with its many corners of strangeness, though one night's sleep here has ironed a few rumples smooth. I know where the bathroom is. O, that immaculate, invisibly renewed *sanitas* of rented bathrooms, inviting us to strip off not merely our clothes and excrement and the particles of overspiced flank steak between our teeth but our skin with the dirt and our circumstances with the skin and then to flush every bit down the toilet the loud voracity of whose flushing action so rebukingly contrasts with the clogged languor of the toilets we have left behind at home, already so full of us they can scarcely ebb! The mirror holds a face. I do not recognize it as mine. It no more fits my inner light than the shade of a bridge lamp fits its bulb.

This lampshade. This lopsided lampshade. This lampshade knocked askew. This sallow sack that time has laundered to the tint of recycled paper, inexpungibly speckled and discolored, paper with nevertheless the droop of melting rubber and the erosion of an aerial view, each of its myriad wrinkles a canyon deep enough to hold all the corpses of the last four decades. Not mine. But it winks when I will, *wink;* it occupies, I see by the mirror, the same volume of space wherein the perspectives at which I perceive various projecting edges of the room would intersect, given an ethereal draughtsman. These teeth are mine. Every filling and inlay is a mournful story I could sing. These eyes—holes of a mask. Through which the blue sky shows as in one of Magritte's eerily outdoor paintings. God's eyes, my lids.

The Reverend Mr. Thomas Marshfield, 41 this April last, 5′ 10″, 158 pounds, pale and neural, yet with unexpected whirlpools of muscularity here and there—the knees, the padding of the palms, a hard collar of something bullish and taut about the base of the neck and the flaring out of the shoulders. Once a shortstop, once a prancing pony of a halfback. Balding now. Pink on top if I tilt for the light, otherwise a gibbonesque halo of bronze fuzz. Mouse tufts above dead white ears. Something ruddy about the tufts; field mice? Little in the way of eyebrows. Little in the way of lips: my mouth, its two wiggles fitted with a wary set as if ready to dart into an ambiguous flurry of expressions, has never pleased me, though it has allegedly pleased others. Chin a touch too long. Nose also, yet thin enough and sufficiently unsteady in its line of descent to avoid any forceful Hebraism of character. A face still uneasily inhabited, by a tenant waiting for his credit ratings to be checked. In this interregnum neither handsome nor commanding, yet at least with nothing plump about it and, lamplike, a latently incandescent willingness to resist what is current. I have never knowingly failed to honor the supreme, the hidden commandment, which is, Take the Natural World, O Creature Fashioned in Parody of My Own, and Reconvert its Stuff to Spirit; Take Pleasure and Make of it Pain; Chastise Innocence though it Reside within the Gaps of the Atom; Suspect Each Moment, for it is a Thief, Tiptoeing Away with More than it Brings; Question all Questions; Doubt all Doubts; Despise all Precepts which Take their Measure from Man; Remember Me.

I am a conservative dresser. Black, gray, brown let the wearer shine. Though I take care with the knot of my tie, I neglect to polish my shoes.

I believe my penis to be of average size. This belief has not been won through to effortlessly.

My digestion is perversely good, and my other internal units function with the smoothness of subversive cell meetings in a country without a government. A translucent wart on my right buttock should some day be removed, and some nights sleep is forestalled by a neuralgic pain in my left arm, just below the shoulder, that I blame upon a bone bruise suffered in a high-school scrimmage. My appendix is unexcised. I feel it, and my heart, as time bombs.

I love myself and loathe myself more than other men. One of these excesses attracts women, but which?

My voice is really a half-octave too high for the ministry, though in praying aloud I have developed a way of murmuring to the lectern mike that answers to my amplified sense of the soliloquizing ego. My slight stammer keeps, they tell me, the pews from nodding.

What else? My wrists ache.

The state I am in is large and square and holds one refugee asthmatic and three drunken Indians in a Ford pickup per square mile. The state I late inhabited, and where I committed my distracted dereliction and underwent my stubborn pangs, has been nibbled by the windings of rivers and deformed by the pull of conflicting territorial claims into an unspecifiable shape, rendered further amorphous by lakes and islands and shelves of urban renewal landfill. A key, Chesterton somewhere says, has no logic to its shape: its only logic is, it turns the lock.

My lord, this depletes the inner man! Thank Heaven for noon.

2

Ms. Prynne tells me to write (I asked, daring halt her headlong progress down a maroon-muffled and slowly curving hall) about what interests me most.

What interests me most, this morning—the image that hangs most luminous and blue amid the speckled leaves of that far-off, shapeless state where I had a profession, a parish, a marriage, and a parsonage, is of a man with chalk-white legs (myself), clad in naught but the top half of pajamas striped like an untwisted candy cane, treading across a frosty post-Hallowe'en lawn. He climbs a waist-high picket fence, and, gingerly as a kudu dipping his muzzle at the edge of a hyena-haunted waterhole, edges his profile, amid bushes, against the glow of the window of a little one-story house, once a parsonage garage.

A man and a woman are in this house. The outside man, also aware of the flirtatious brushing of

Japanese yew needles on his exposed buttocks (he goes to bed without the pajama bottoms for at least a trinity of reasons: to facilitate masturbatory self-access, to avoid belly-bind due to drawstrings or buttons, to send an encouraging signal to the mini-skirted female who, having bitten a poisoned apple at the moment of my father's progenitive orgasm, lies suspended within me), knew this. He knew her car, a rotund black coupe of American vintage. He saw her car, gazing from the window of his bedroom, parked an alley away, visible through the naked branches of trees that (deciduousness! already I mourn for thee) in summer would have concealed its painful placement. The hooked gleam from its scarab back, purple beneath the sulphurous streetlight that brooded above the alley, went straight as steel to his heart. For an hour or more he writhed, this fabulous far-off man (whom I vow will not be forgotten, though all the forces of institutional therapeutics be brought to bear upon me in this diabolical air-conditioned sandbox) trying to worm the harpoon from its lodging in his silvery, idden [*sic*] underside. He masturbated again, imagining for spite some woman remote, a redhead from the attic of his youth, her pubic hair as nicely packed around its treasure as excelsior around an ancestral locket. For a moment, after his poor throttled accomplice had yielded again its potent loot, the bed under him sagged into grateful nonsense and he thought he might slip through the jostle of jealousy into sleep. Then the image of her car under its streetlight returned, and the thought of her cries under caresses, and of her skin under clothes, and of her voice under silence—for there was no doubting, this act of hers addressed itself to *him*. For she was his mistress and that same week had lain with him.

He arose from the bed. His wife adjusted her position within the great gray egg of her unconsciousness. He did not dare test the creak-prone closet door; clad as partially as when he arose, he made his way down oaken staircases flayed with moonbeams to a front door whose fanlight held in Byzantine rigidity the ghosts of its Tiffany colors. A-tremble—his whole body one large tremble, only solid seemingly, like solid matter—he pressed his thumb upon the concussive latch, eased the towering giant of a parsonage portal toward his twittering chest, stepped outside, onto granite, and bathed his legs in wintry air.

This is fun! First you whittle the puppets, then you move them around.

The lawn was frosty. The neighborhood was dark. The moon peered crookedly over his shoulder, curious enough to tilt its head. The Reverend Mr. Marshfield avoided stepping on the fragments of a Wiffle Ball his sons had ragefully fragmented, on a can his dog had chewed and savored like a bone, on the glinting pieplate of clothespins his wife, dear sainted sloven, had neglected to bring in from some autumnal drying—the white sheets whipping, the last swirled exodus of starlings peppering the flavorless sky. That was ago. This was now. Once upon a time the secret stars of frost winked out beneath his soles. He foresaw the fence, even remembered the bill (typed with a brown ribbon) from the contractor (a lugubrious cheat, long since bankrupted) who planted it there by vote of the board of deacons (Gerald Harlow, chairman), picked for his tread a spot in the frozen flower border where no old rose clippings might have speared him ("With the help of the thorn in my foot," Kierkegaard wrote, "I spring higher than anyone with sound feet"), and in one smooth parabolic step our ex-athletic cleric and voyeur swung his ungirded loins an airy inch or so above the pointed painted pickets and with cold toes trespassed upon the ill-tended turf of his assistant minister, effeminate, bearded Ned (for Thaddeus, somehow) Bork.

Perfidy, thy name might as well be Bork. The present writer, his nose and eyeballs still stinging from his first afternoon of desert brightness, can scarcely locate what is most signally odious about this far-away young man. His unctuous, melodious, prep-school drawl? His rosy cheeks? His hint of acne? The chestnut curls of his preening beard? His frog-colored eyes? Or was it his limp-wristed theology, a perfectly custardly confection of Jungian-Reichian soma-mysticism swimming in a soupy caramel of Tillichic, Jasperian, Bultmannish blather, all served up in a dime-store dish of his gutless generation's give-away Gemütlichkeit? His infectious giggle? Or the fact that everybody in the parish, from the puling baptizee to the terminal crone hissing in the oxygen tent, loved him?

Actually, I liked him too.

And wanted him to like me.

He was in there with my carnal love. I crept from window to window, meeting tactile differentiations among the variety of shrubs the local nursery (which piously kept its Puerto Rican peony-pluckers in a state of purposeful peonage) had donated to our holy cause of parsonage improvement. They were in this garage renovated to bachelor's quarters, my organist and my curate, one of each sex, like interlocked earrings in a box too large for such storage. But one dim light shone within Bork's quarters. His rooms, though not many and all on one floor, were arranged with a maddening cleverness; from whatever window I, my nakedness clawed, stealthily scrambled to, the shuffle of partitions eclipsed what I needed to see. The paper cutouts in my hollow Easter egg had fallen all to one side and presented only blurry one-dimensional edges. Yet I could hear, in the gaps between the crackling thunder of my feet and the ponderous surf of my breathing, voices—or, if not quite voices, then the faint rubbed spot on the surface of silence that indicates where voices have been erased.

Fearful lest the hypothetical passing patrol car spot me, the ideal bare-bummed burglar, I eased to the alley and peered in the window to the left of the front door; at the other extreme of the tiny house's immense space, by the light of a lamp that seemed to be muffled beneath rose-colored blankets, I beheld a white triangle, quick as a Nikon's shutter, flesh* above the edge of a sofa, and vanish as quickly from view. Too sharp to be a knee, it must have been an elbow. Too fair to be his, it must have been hers. She was above him, in the position of Hera and Zeus, of Shakti and Shiva. More power to the peephole!

The glimpse burned in me like a drop of brandy in the belly of an ostensibly reformed alcoholic. I crept, literally ("upon thy belly shalt thou go"), through the icy grass beneath the sills of the side windows to the window nearest the sofa. With a wariness that made my joints petition against gradualism I straightened enough to peek in a lower pane. Though dwelling in outer darkness, I might be caught by the flare of a match or by a shouting** star, and anyway felt my face to be burning like a banshee's. I let one bulged eye look on behalf of both.

There, not a man's length away, basking in pinkish glow, lay a bare foot. Hers. Alicia had homely feet, veinous and glazed on the knuckles of some

* I of course meant to type "flash."

** O.K. C*f*. Wm. Blake.

toes as if primed for an appliqué of corns. This was a foot of hers. Irrefutably. And irrefutably naked. I was stunned. I listened for the cries it was her wont wantonly to emit in coitus. But Bork, like so many of his carefree-seeming generation, had a sharp lookout on his own comfort, and had put up his storm windows. Then, before my face, at just the other side of the double installment of glass, there was a commotion of hair, his or hers I couldn't tell, so instantaneous was my flinching, and my subsequent rolling downwards and sideways into the lee of a comradely bush that from the well-oiled prickle of its leaves must have been a holly. Cretinous and cunning as an armadillo, I lay there bathed in mulch chips until I deemed the stillness safe for a dancing retreat—my legs scribbling like chalk on a blackboard—across Bork's moon-hard lawn into the creaky, fusty forgiveness of my fanlighted foyer.

No sirens had arisen in the night to pursue me.

No angels materialized on the staircase.

Moonbeams still lay across it like stripes on the bent brown back of a suppliant slave.

Within myself, under the caked hot crusty sensation that arises to shield us from athletic defeat and direct insult, I felt horror at my visual confirmation of the already evidentially (given the parked car, the house, the hour, the ubiquity of sex, and the infallible Providence that arranges for my discomfort) certain. But, twinned with horror and bedded snugly beside it, a warm body of satisfaction lay detectable within myself. This pleasure, though alloyed, was deep, deeper than the half-believer's masochism, deeper than my truffler's hunger for secrets, of which the bare foot was now one. So deep, indeed, that, gazing down, from within the warm stairwell alive with the ticking of my rent-free radiators, I saw the comfortable carpets and shadow-striped floor of my father's house, also not his own.

But the hands of the motel clock have already moved past the crowing erectitude of noon. Today, I think, a Daiquiri, with an icing of suds atop the soothing rum, and then another.

And first we must move our bare-legged puppet up the stairs and put him to bed. He presses open the bedroom door with a barely perceptible snap that nevertheless, he knows, snaps his wife's eyes open.

"My God. Tom. Where have you been?"

"Checking on the children. Putting out the cat."

He slithers into his vacated place, shoving to one side the warm fragments of herself that she allowed to spill there. She asks, "Why are your feet so cold? And your bottom? You're freezing."

"I was out on the lawn."

"With no pants on?"

"I was looking for UFOs."

"I don't believe it."

"Also the paper said there was going to be a comet. Or some such heavenly portent."

"I don't believe it. You were spying on Ned. That's sick."

"He's in my cure of souls. *Curo, curate, curare.*"

"Tom, that is sick. What are we going to do with you?"

And I thought for an abysmal second she, her hand surveying my coldness, was going to fumble for my penis. But the danger, as do so many, passed.

3

My father's house house house hou

Fingers droop above the keys, the shiny print above this desk (a Remingtonesque work depicting a horse, a bush, and a sod hut all basking in a prairie sunset too cerise to be true) develops fascinating details (is that an elbow protruding from one window? is that a fissure or a river off to the left?), and incidents of yesterday's golf match return to me plaguingly. After swinging with a nice clicking freedom from tee to green, in the thin air, in the cactoid terrain, I missed three consecutive putts of less than three feet, indicating either emergent astigmatism or a severe character defect. The sense of that ball, so anxiously tapped, sliding by on the high side and hanging there as obdurately as the fact of pain in the world: it pulls one's insides quite awry. Disbelief warps us so that tears are nearly wrung from our ducts. Red fury rolls in. Perdition! Perdition to the universe of which this hole is the off-center center! All men hate God, Melville says.

My father's house was several houses, as he moved from parish to parish, but the furniture remained the same, and the curved feet, not leonine but paws without claws, without toes, of a mahogany-veneered highboy return large to me, as something that must have engaged my fancy when a crawler. The nap of the Oriental rug, upon whose edge of angular blue flowers these impossibly round feet intruded, was exceptionally lush at the edges, and ominously threadbare where the feet of our family and my father's visitors trod.

They would mumble behind his study door, the visitors. On Saturdays he would type—ejaculations of clatter after long foreplay of silent agony. These sounds of ministerial activity engraved themselves upon a deadly silence. My father and my mother said little. They had few friends to whom he was not a nuncio from a better world. I was the youngest of four children, but the brother nearest me, Stephen, was light-years older than I, and away at school from the time I could toddle. I had been a kind of afterthought, a mistake. My very existence was some sort of jape. I apologized the best I could, by being good. Though the library was lined with books that mingled Heaven with our daily dust, none could explain the riddle of my existence. It lay within my mother. My mother had once been fair; fair, turning sepia with age, her image gazed from the living-room mantel—from the succession of living-room mantels. It was among the treasures I had to claim when she died of lung cancer seven years ago, and I was struck by how small it was, this image, and how conventional, with that high-browed, absent-eyed blur of beauties before World War I. In the end, fashion overcomes personality: all the mistresses of Louis XV look alike. My mother once had a beautiful voice, but by the time I was big enough to stand beside her in church, her voice had been hoarsened by time and chronic bronchitis, and as if in protest she would stand silent beside me, following the words in the hymnal with her eyes, but her mouth softly closed, her silence pealing in my heart. From their bedroom, too, silence, once the mumble of my father's account of their day died, and with it the lighter music, mostly rests, of my mother's responses, and her voluntary canticle of the household, a few chimed facts that primarily, I imagined, concerned me. Then, silence. So my pleasure in verifying that Ned and Alicia were screwing might be, deeply, pleasure in discovering that my parents in their silence were not dead but alive, that my birth had not chilled all love, that the bower of their union continued to flourish above me.

These sentences have come in no special order. Each of them has hurt. Each might have been different, with the same net effect. All facts are equivalently dismal. Any set of circumstances can give rise to a variety of psychological conditions. We acknowledge this when we skip the flashbacks in novels.

Rereading, I see that my mother's singing voice was, for me, her sex; that her hoarseness I transferred in my childish innocence to her lower mouth, which was, as I stood small beside her in the pew, at the level of my mouth; that I equate noise with vitality; that silence, chastity, and death fascinate me with one face; that Alicia's power over the organ keyboards was part of her power over me.

I see that, meaning to write about my father, I have written about my mother instead. Yet she was insignificant, timid, mousily malcontented, immense only in the dimension of time, of constancy. Whereas my father was an impressive, handsome figure, and is so even now, at the age of seventy-seven, sitting senile in a nursing home.

And I notice that I wrote "by being good" when I should have written "by lying low"—for there is a curiously serpentine altitude to not only my infantile impressions but to those received when I had straightened up, even when I had grown to my mother's height. Her hymn book is always above the level of my eyes, and I feel before me the space *under* the pew, with its never-varnished wood and unhemmed edges of velvet held by old-fashioned upholsterer's tacks, their brass heads tarnished to the color of a dried bloodstain. "He who is down," we used to sing, "need fear no fall." "All they that go down to the dust," quoth the Psalmist, "shall bow before Him." Sexually speaking (and why not? school's out) I preferred the inferior position—on top, the woman is so much more supple and knobby and *interested*—and adored "going down." O, how Alicia's exclamations, sweeter than honey in the hive, would resound in my ears as they were clamped in the sticky, warm, living vise of her thighs! And down beyond down, those toes, so well described yesterday, what rapture it gave me to kiss them, especially when the smell of sweat and Capezio leather lay secret on their skin or, of a barefooted summer day, sand and salt and the flavor of the innumerable trod particles, from tar-crumb to dead-leaf-flake, that comprise the blessed ground of our being!

The Tillichian pun comes opportunely. For I need still to say, what scrambles the keys to say, that my father's house bred into me a belief in God, which has made my life one long glad feast of inconvenience and unreason.

How did it do this?

How did I manage to gather such a monstrous impression?

That my father, as he pottered about intending to wag the world with the stubby scruffy tail of his stuffy congregation, appeared dim-witted to me, I have already implied. He was not a wise nor, insofar as his public commitment to be exemplary inflicted a mousy tyranny upon his household, a kind man. He was at his best (hel*low* again) in his basement, in the succession of our basements, where he would establish a workbench of phenomenal neatness, the hammers and pliers and calipers placed upon their outlines painted on pegboard, the well-oiled tablesaw (its absolutely level metal top my first vision of rectitude) established on the right, and the cans of paint and putty and solvent shelved on the left, and the jars of nails and screws of progressive and labelled sizes nailed by their lids to a board above; and there my father would spend part of most afternoons, performing, in the warmth of the proximate furnace, small tasks of mending and manufacture that, to my childish sense, were meaningless but for the meaning the shavings breathed, and the cleansing aroma of the turpentine, and the inner peace emanating from my puttering, pipe-smoking, fussy, oblivious father. I would sit on a sawhorse and love my upward view of his cleft chin, his vital nostrils, his wavy gray hair—its brushed luxuriance his one overt vanity.

I did not confuse my father and God. I knew it was not God in that basement, but an underpaid, rather loosely instructed employee. Nor was God in the churches, save rarely, as when a bass organ note left pedalled from the Amen rattled the leading of the apostles' stained-glass haloes and echoed from the darkest, not-even-at-Easter-inhabited rear of the balcony like a waking animal groaning from his burrow. In general the churches, visited by me too often on weekdays—when the custodian was moving the communion table about like a packing case, and sweeping up the chewing-gum wrappers that insolently spangled the sacrosanct reaches of the choir—bore for me the same relation to God that billboards did to Coca-Cola: they promoted thirst without quenching it.

But it was, somehow, and my descriptive zeal flags, in the *furniture* I awoke among, and learned to walk among, and fell asleep amid—it was the moldings of the doorways and the sashes of the windows and the turning of the balusters—it was the carpets each furry strand of which partook in a pattern and the ceilings whose random cracks and faint discolorations I would never grow to reach, that convinced me, that *told* me, God was, and was here, even as the furnace came on, and breathed gaseous warmth upon my bare, buttonshoed legs. Someone invisible had cared to make these things. There was a mantel clock, with a face of silver scrolls, that ticked and gonged time which would at the last gong end, and the dead would awake, and a new time would begin. Beyond the stairs, there were invisible stairs leading unimaginably upward. There was a sofa where I would, older, lie and eat raisins and read O. Henry and John Tunis and Admiral Byrd and dream; the sofa itself felt to be dreaming; it was stuffed with the substance of the spirit.

Though we had moved, following my father's call, from one city of inland America to another, this sofa was a constant island, and the furniture a constant proof of, as it were, a teleologic bias in things, a temporary slant as of an envelope halfway down the darkness inside a mailbox.

Not much of a *point de départ pour le croyant qui souffre,* eh? Not even the grand Argument from Design, for it has taken me forty of my years to begin to transfer my sense of the Divine outdoors. Sunsets, mountaintops, lake surfaces rippling like silk in the wind, all strike me as having the faintly fraudulent splashiness of churches, a forced immanence. Athletic fields and golf courses excepted, the out-of-doors wears an evil aspect, dominated as it is by insects and the brainless proliferation of vegetable forms. Little grits and small fittings are crags and dells enough for my pantheism.

(Pascal dreaded landscapes too. How I do crave the *Pensées!* The squaw at the commissary let me have a John Dickson Carr and a P. G. Wodehouse, but when I gingerly asked if there was any Dorothy Sayers, she blushed as wickedly as if I had asked for the *Summa Theologica.*)

To sum up, and to bring my day's trial to an end, I had no choice but to follow my father into the ministry; the furniture forced me to do it. I became a Barthian, in reaction against his liberalism, a smiling fumbling shadow of German Pietism, of Hegel's and Schleiermacher's and Ritschl's polywebbed attempt to have it all ways, of those doddering Anglican empiricists who contribute the theological articles to the Encyclopaedia Britannica (no mention of Kierkegaard! of Baudelaire! of the Grand Inquisitor! where is the leap! the abyss! the black credibility of the *deus absconditus!* instead, a fine-fingered finicking indistinguishable in texture from the flanking articles on pond biomorphs and macromolecules), which stance in turn had been taken, in defiance of hellfire, out of reaction to his own father, an anti-Darwinian fundamentalist, a barrel-thumping revivalist risen repentant from the swamps of pioneer booze. No doubt these nuances matter less than we in the trade imagine.

And no doubt one Daiquiri less before lunch will do wonders for my sunstruck short putts after. That little Tennessean, a closet sodomist if I read his body-language aright, is deadly from six feet in.

No. Two points arose as I rummaged in the bathroom for the Coppertone. One, I did not become a Barthian in blank recoil, but in positive love of Barth's voice, his wholly masculine, wholly informed, wholly unfrightened prose. In his prose thorns become edible, as for the giraffe. In Barth I heard, at the age of eighteen, the voice my father should have had.

Two, my intuition about objects is thus the exact opposite of that of Robbe-Grillet, who intuits (transcription of a bird call: *in-tu-it, in-too-eeet*) in tables, rooms, corners, knives, etc., an emptiness resounding with the universal nullity. He has only to describe a chair for us to know that God is absent. Whereas for me, puttying a window sash, bending my face close in, awakens a plain suspicion that someone in the immediate vicinity immensely, discreetly cares. God. Since before language dawned I knew what the word meant: all haggling as to this is linguistic sophistry. "Bending my face close in" reminds me (if you care, supposed reader, about this kind of connection) of that redhead some pages and more years ago, "her pubic hair as nicely packed around its treasure as excelsior around an ancestral locket." An attic closeness. I wonder, truly, if "love" (old whore of a word, we'll let you in this once, fumigated by quotation marks) is not a reifying rather than de-reifying process, and "sex object" not the summit of homage.

Away with personhood! Mop up spilt religion! Let us have it in its original stony jars or not at all!

4

I inherited her. Alicia had been hired by my predecessor, a languid gnostic stirred to dynamism only by the numen of church finances. Having ministered to our flock and its fleece during the go-go years, he left me a fat portfolio and lean attendance rolls. I was told, indeed, that the Reverend Morse believed that nothing so became a parishioner's life as the leaving of it, with a valedictory bequest to the building fund. More, *mors*! At any rate the nominal members stayed away from the sabbath pews as from an internal revenue inquisitor, until the word went about in the land that lo! the new parson was not a hunting one, but a hunted. O, shame upon me as I recall those Sundays in the world, my sermons so fetchingly agonized, so fashionably antinomian. I suffered, impaled upon those impossible texts, weeping tears with my refusal to blink at the eschatological, yet happy in my work, pale in my pantomime of holy agitation, self-pleasing in my sleepless sweat, a fevered scapegoat taking upon myself the sins of the prosperous. The blue-suited businessmen regarded me with guarded but approbatory grimace as a curious sort of specialist, while musk arose thicker than incense from between the legs of their seated wives. But enough of such shoptalk. I was sincere, if the word has meaning. Better our own act than another's. The Lord smiled; the cloud of witnesses beneath me grew, while wiring hung inside the pulpit like entrails in a butcher's shop, and my collection of interior pornography improved in technical quality (the early graininess expunged by computer-enhancement from these latest Danish imports), and the organ behind me pertly sliced a premature end to the eloquent anguish of my prayerful pause.

She was pert, short, nearsighted, blonde in the hard ironed style, argumentative, and rather metronomic. My organist at the previous church had been a plump black man who rolled on the bench like a flywheel and set the pews to swaying during collection so freely the plates hopped from hand to hand like the bouncing ball at a sing-along. Sweeping the floors became a franchise, there was so much dropped change. Alicia, why do you keep hiding behind these wisecracks? When you sat down to play, I wondered if the thick soles of your trendy shoes wouldn't keep you from pedalling properly. Chartreuse bell-bottoms peeked from beneath your cassock. Behind your tinted octagonal spectacles, were your red-rimmed rabbit eyes really so shifty? I found out, didn't I?

"Mrs. Crick, did you feel you might have taken 'A Mighty Fortress' a shade fast?" She is divorced, with two small children. Hire the handicapped. Her age on the edge of thirty, as mine is on that of forty. Those ten years up on me, and the contemplative pout of her lips, stiff as a sugar rose, and the impudent monocle-flash of one or the other of her spectacles as she tips her glossy head goad me to add, " 'A *Flighty* Fortress,' we should call it. Your tempo left the choir procession stranded halfway down the aisle."

"The children's choir dawdled filing out," is Mrs. Crick's response. And: "You can't drag every hymn just because it's religious."

In retrospect, and no doubt then as well, beneath my risen hackles, I loved her standing up to me. Life, that's what we seek in one another, even with the DNA molecule cracked and our vitality arraigned before us as a tiny Tinkertoy.

"There's such a thing as feeling," I told her.

"And such a thing as feigning," she responded.

Why can't I keep this in the present tense? She recedes in the vaults of the past as, on many a night, the clatter of the choristers having faded in a wash of headlights, she would switch off the organ (a 1920 three-manual electro-pneumatic, with a thrillingly discordant calliope of mixture stops), gather to her breasts her *Sämtliche Orgelwerke von Dietrich Buxtehude* and *Oeuvres complètes pour Orgue de J. S. Bach annotées et doigtées par Marcel Dupré* and *99 Tabernacle Favorites for Choir & Organ,* and sigh and recede down the dimmed and silenced nave to the lancet doors and the black car parked in the black lot beyond.

"Good-night, Mrs. Crick."

"Good-night, Reverend Marshfield."

The draft from her opening the door arrived at my ankles as the sound of its closing arrived at my ears. I feel my cassock sway in this wind. It is dead winter. Reverend. A chill. Her blonde shimmer receding down the aisle, shifting into murky brunette. Her bottom, in adherent slacks, surprisingly ample and expressive. A touch of sorrow rounding her shoulders. Her dumpy old Chevrolet. I knew little about her life apart from Thursday nights and Sunday mornings. She gave piano lessons in the neighboring suburb. She had two children, who did not come to Sunday school. She must have lovers.

"You are implying," I said above, after her "feigning," "what?" My wariness was not only that of the watcher but that of the watched. For some time, her attention had been upon me: my hackles knew it.

She sat on the arm of a pew and hugged her pastel sheaf of music tighter. In this strained position her knees, bonier than the rest of her, protruded and pressed white edges into the stretchy knit of her tights. Was she about to weep? Her voice was dry. "I'm sorry. I don't know what I was implying. You're a good man. No, you're not. I'm sorry, I don't have any control over what I'm saying. Something else has upset me, not you."

"Would you like to tell me what?" I asked, though it was more about me, her image of me, that I wanted to hear.

"Oh, some man."

"Who won't marry you?"

She looked up, her eyes behind the tinted lenses pink and worn. "That must be it," she said, sarcastically.

"I'm wrong," I offered.

"You're close enough." Her head bowed again. "You just get so tired," she added, of another "you," in weak apology.

Her life, the Gothic carpentry of the church, the night and town outside, the parish and its tired, teeming life all as in an Uccello converged on this sadness; I was in a black center, a mildew-darkened patch on a mural; I was conscious of my white hands, posed anxiously before me as if trying to build a house of cards in the air. Their palms tingled. Her bowed head glowed. To this moment, toward which four decades narrowed, I had never been unfaithful to my wife. There had been temptations as strong, but my will to be tempted had been weaker.

"Tired of what? Tell me."

She lifted her face; her face was behind glass.

What do I mean, writing that? Am I imposing backwards upon the moment the later moment when truly she was behind glass, her foot and her hair, with Ned? Or did my knowledge that a process of seduction was at work, that this face could, if not now, later, be touched, secrete in panic a transparent barrier? Her jaw wore a curious, arrogant, cheap, arrested set, as if about to chew gum. "Of men," she said, interrogatively—"?" The lift in her voice leaving the sentence open was an offering. She clamped it shut after a pause. "You'd be shocked if I told you."

I did not dispute. Dinna press, when swinging a club or parrying with a woman. Let the club do the work. I may have resolved, also, in this pocket of my silence, to make her pay later for this snub of hers; or again this cruel notion may be imposed in retrospect, a later loop of the film overlapping.

"Then tell me about *me*," said I, bold and insouciant, a modern cleric, perching on the arm of a pew opposite. The prim wood nipped my buttocks. "I'm not a good man," I rehearsed my prey. "I feign."

As I had hoped, she became argumentative.

" 'Good,' " she took up. "I don't understand goodness. The term doesn't have much meaning for me. Things happen, people do things, and that's it. I know you don't believe that. I *do* think you exaggerate yourself as a believing unbeliever, as a man sweating it out on the edge of eternity or whatever; you *tease* the congregation. You shouldn't. Those people out there, they're just dumb; they don't know why they're hurting, or going into bankruptcy, or knocked-up, or lonely, or whatever. You shouldn't act out your personal psychodrama on their time. I mean, this isn't meant to be your show, it's *theirs.*"

"I see," I said, lying.

She saw I was. "I mean," she said, and I loved the flush of earnestness stealing that street-wise gum-chewing cool from her features, "don't be so angry, about patterns and obstacles that are all in your head."

"Angry? Am I?"

"I'd say," Alicia said, "you're the angriest *sane* man I've ever met."

So you've met angry insane men? But I didn't ask that; I asked, benevolently, "What do you think I'm angry about?"

"What we're all angry about. You're unhappy."

Still smiling, still stoking my smile with interior vows of revenge, I asked, inevitably, "And what makes me so unhappy?"

I assumed she would answer, *Your theology*. Instead she said, "Your marriage."

"Isn't it perfect?" I asked; the words, inane yet divinely enunciated, arose beyond me, in some dictionary seraphim update.

My dear sexy organist laughed. Her laugh filled the church like golden mud—or do I misquote? "It's *ter*rible," she propounced,* myopic and merry and her kneecaps thrust into anxious relief by some stress in her perching position. "It's worse than mine even, and that didn't last three years!"

There is a Biblical phrase whose truth I then lived: scales fell from my eyes. She was right. In her helmet of centrally cleft floss this angel had come and with a blazing sword slashed the gray (as cardboard, as brain cells) walls of my prison.

This conversation took place early in Lent; I kissed her in the vestibule the evening of Holy Saturday, between the lancet doors giving inward on the nave and the weatherstripped doors giving outward on the expectant night, gathering her into my arms above the wire rack of Lenten pamphlets and appropriate versicles directed at the alcoholic, the lonely, the doubtful, the estranged, gathering into my arms a startling, agitated, conflicted, uneven mix of softnesses and hardnesses, warm spots and cool, her body. After Easter, her veteran Chevrolet Providentially having torn a gasket, she let me drive her home, and took me upstairs to her surprisingly ample bed.

* Let it ride.

Perhaps the conversation as I have set it down is a medley of several, scattered through a number of post- or pre-rehearsal interludes, in drafty ecclesiastic nooks haunted by whiffs of liquid wax and spilled cider, or on awkward frozen lawns while our gloved hands groped for the handles of differing automobiles (mine a coffee-brown 1971 Dodge Dart, hers a 1963, if memory serves, Bel Air).

Or perhaps these words were never spoken, I made them up, to relieve and rebuke the silence of this officiously chaste room.

5

Alicia in bed was a revelation. At last I confronted as in an ecstatic mirror my own sexual demon. In such a hurry we did not always take time to remove socks and necklaces and underthings that clung to us then like shards or epaulettes, we would tumble upon her low square bed, whose headboard was a rectangle of teak and whose bedspread a quiltwork sunburst, and she would push me down and, her right hand splayed on her belly, tugging upward the tarnished gift of her pubic fur so as to make an unwispy fit, would seat herself upon my upraised* phallus, whose mettle she had firmed with fingers and lips, and whimper, and come, and squirm, and come again, her vaginal secretions so copious my once-too-sensitive glans slid through its element calm as a fish, and politely declined to ejaculate, so

* The first time, believe it or not, I typed "unpraised"—my uxorious lament in an uninvited consonant.

that she came once more, and her naked joy, witnessed, forced a laugh from my chest. Such laughing was unprecedented for me; under my good wife's administration sex had been a solemn, once-a-week business, ritualized and worrisomely hushed.

The minx's breasts were small but smartly tipped, her waist comfortably thick, her feet homely as I have said and well-used-looking, as were her active hands, all muscle and bone, and her pubic patch the curious no-color of tarnish, of gilt dulled to the edge of brown, the high note of her blonde head transposed to a seductive minor.

That musical metaphor brought, just now, me to a treacherous pitch—see earlier, the "saving grace note upon the baffled chord of self." I jerked off, lying on the wall-to-wall carpet of goose-turd green, rather than sully my bachelor cot where the Navajo chambermaid might sardonically note the spoor of a wounded paleface. My seed sank into polyester lint and the microscopic desert grits of a hundred transient shoes. I shouldn't have done it, for now my hymn to my mistress will be limp and piecemeal, tapped out half by a hand still tremulous and smelling of venerable slime.

At the join of Alicia's abdomen and thighs you could count the tendrils one by one; they thickened in the center to a virtual beard that, when we showered together ere returning to the scoured world, she would let me shape with soap into a jaunty goatee. She loved her own cunt, handled it and crooned of it as if it were, not the means to a child, but a child itself, tender and tiny and intricate and mischievously willful. "My trouble is," she told me, "I think with my cunt." "I'm kissing my own cunt!" she sighed unforgettably once when I fetched my mouth fresh from below and pressed it wet upon her own. The lover as viaduct. The lover as sky-god, cycling moisture from earth to cloud to earth.

Though she was a fair enough sky herself. We played in each other like children in puddles. Dabbled and stared, dabbled and stared. The mud of her, white and rose and gold, reflected blue zenith.

Play. There was that, in daylight, laughing, after a marriage bed of nighttime solemnity and spilt religion, spilt usually at the wrong angle, at the moment when the cup had been withdrawn. What fun my forgotten old body turned out to be—the toy I should have been given for Christmas, instead of the jack-in-the-box, or the little trapeze artist between his squeezable sticks, or the Lionel locomotive entering and re-entering his papier-mâché tunnel. Thank you, playmate, for such a light-headed snowy morning, your own body more baubled than a Christmas tree, with more vistas to it than within a kaleidoscope. In holiday truth my wonder did seem to rebound upon you, merry, merry, and make you chime.

Play, and pain. Her moans, her cries, at first frightened me, at the very first because I naïvely imagined I was in my newfound might hurting her ("You're wombing me!" she once cried, astraddle) and next because I feared such depth of pleasure was not enough my creation, was too much hers, and could too easily be shifted to the agency of another. There is this to be said for cold women; they stick. So beneath our raptures I heard the tearing silk of infidelity, and she heard the ticking clock that would lift me, from whatever height of self-forgetfulness, on to the next appointment, and home, to check the patch of invisible mending on my absence. Alicia found it hard to let me go, I know. For I was a rare man, in this latter world of over-experienced men. Her bestowals had not for some years, I judged, won such gratitude and ardor. So my swift resumption of my suit of black, even to rubber overshoes in the post-Paschal season of slush, caused all of her skin, bare on our bed, to stare amazed. Her clinging to me naked, at the head of the stairs, is the only embrace it displeases me to recall. Though the sight of her, then, I turning for one last, upward glance, the stairs descended, her legs cut off at the ankle and her propping arms "bled" from the rectangle framing her silhouette, the sight of her, I say, before I turned and pulled open the barking door to the breezy world, still so moves this abandoning heart that a less tension-loving typist would be driven again to the ruggy floor of his padded cell.

Play, and pain, and display. Her house was a little peach-colored one in a row of varicolored but otherwise uniform houses on a curved street so newly scraped into being that mud ran red in the gutters when it rained and the only trees were staked saplings. The upstairs windows were dormered; her children each had a small room facing front and Alicia had taken for herself the long room giving on the back yard, with its brave spindle of an infant beech, and an incipient box hedge, and her garage, and an alley where an oil truck seemed often to be idly churning, and the bleak backs of the next street in the development. Across a tract of purple woods waiting for their development stood what appeared to be an abandoned gravel pit and, on the crest above it, incongruously, the little spikes and buttons of tombstones in a cemetery, where I had, I believed, a few times, buried souls. I loved this sparse, raw neighborhood, for its impoverished air suggested that Alicia did not have the means to leave me, however often I briskly dressed and left her, and its lack of trees—the opposite of my own heavily oaked and elmed neighborhood of imposing McKinley-vintage manses—let the light in unclouded, nude as ourselves, and like us eternally young. O Alicia, my mistress, my colleague, my adviser, my betrayer, what would I not give—a hand? no, not even a finger, but perhaps the ring from my finger—to see you again mounted at the base of my belly, your shoulders caped with sunshine, your head flung back so your jawbone traced its own omega, your hair on false fire, your breasts hung undefended upon the dainty cage of your ribs and anxious for any mouth to tease them, any hand to touch them, but untouched taking pleasure, it seemed, in their own unresisted swaying, in the wash of light. I lifted my back, the muscles in my thighs pulled, my face was fed, you moaned. We bent a world of curves above the soaked knot where our roots merged.

Alicia was nearsighted, and had to look closely. Else, but for my voice and smell, I was a mist of maleness to her. And I, I borrowed courage from her shamelessness, and looked my fill, and reduced under the caresses of my eyes her pores, striations, wrinkles, wobbles, calluses, and widening flaws—time was making familiar with her, younger than I though she was—to the service of love. That lame word again. I meant to describe "display." Precisely, I worshipped her, adored her flaws as furiously as her perfections, for they were hers; and thus I attained, in the bound of a few spring weeks, a few illicit lays, the attitude which saints bear toward God, and which I in a Christ's lifetime of trying (40 [present age] minus 7 [age of reason] equals 33) had failed to reach, that is, of forgiving Him the pain of infants, the inexorability of disease, the wantonness of fortune, the billions of fossilized deaths, the helplessness of the young, the idiocy of the old, the craftsmanship of torturers, the authority of blunderers, the savagery of accident, the unbreathability of water, and all the other repulsive flecks on the face of Creation.

We preened for each other, posed, danced, socketed every dubious elbow in an avid French kiss of acceptance. You've read it before (I *do* feel someone is reading these pages, though they have the same position on the desk when I return from golf, and my cunning telltales arranged with hairs and paper clips have remained untripped), I know. Skin is an agreeable texture. Penises and vaginas notably so, patent pending. Weaning was an incomplete process. Sex can be fun.

Still, what a relief to have *intelligere* become *esse*. Land ho! She appeared to me during those afternoons of copulation as a promontory on some hitherto sunken continent of light. I had to drive from her town to mine along a highway that, once threaded shadily through fields and pastures, was now straightened, thickened, and jammed with shopping malls, car lots, gas stations, hero sandwich parlors, auto parts paradises, driving ranges, joyless joyrides for the groggy offspring of deranged shoppers, go-go bars windowless as mausoleums (Gay Nite Tuesdays, Cum in Drag), drive-in insurance agencies, the whole gaudy ghastly gasoline-powered consumerish smear, bubbling like tar in the heat of high summer. Yet how washed and constellated it all looked in the aftermath of my sinning! How the fallen world sparkled, now that my faith was decisively lost!

Back from golf (not bad: 94, with only two three-putt greens, and I'm beginning to judge the approach distances better; take two clubs longer than you think, in this deceptive heaven of superair) I feel I should qualify that last rather swanky clause. I brim still, alas, with faith. But Alicia did induce reorientation, of maybe 10°. Imagine me as a circle divided in half, half white and half black. In the white side were such things as my father's furniture, Karl Barth's prose, the fine-grained pliancy and gleeful dependence of my sons* when they were babies, my own crisp hieratic place within the liturgy and sacraments, a secular sense of order within my middle-class life (appointments, meetings, paternity, household and automotive maintenance, falling asleep beside mine *ux.* after the ten o'clock news), certain stray few moments of whiskey and weather, and, on Sundays, the funny papers. This was the Good. I credited God with being on this side. On the other side, the black, which might be labelled the Depressing rather than Evil, lay Mankind (both as a biological species devouring the globe and as those few hundred specimens of it which fell within my ministry—and a cloying, banal, pitiable, mean-

* "See, the smell of my son is as the smell of a field which the Lord hath blessed"—Genesis.

spirited, earthbound repetitive lot they were), my own rank body, most institutional and political trends since 1965, the general decadent trend of the globe, time in all its manifestations, pain, food, books, and all the rest of the Sunday newspaper. Well (an itchy word signalling my increasingly vivid anticipations of a shower, a Whiskey Sour, a lulling view of tinted wasteland, and the blameless friction of male chaffing), Alicia, by reclaiming a wedge of mankind for the Good and Beautiful, shifted the axis of the divider 10° (rough estimate) and caused a relabelling of the now-tilted halves: the white was the Live, the black was the Dead. Most of the ingredients were unaffected by the realignment. God, who has His way of siding with the winners, took Life as His element, and continued to audit my prayers and supervise my digestion as before. Everything not-God, indeed, being dead, gave Him a freer hand. But there was one casualty: in the wedge of the circle directly across from Alicia and her peachy cries and floating nipples was an innocuous sector labelled "*ux.*," inhabited by my wife Jane, née Chillingworth. This wedge went dark as an attic window.

6

Today is Sunday. Though they try to hide this from us, I can count; I came here on a Monday flight, and this is my sixth morning. I must preach. But without a Bible, without a copious and insipid encyclopedia of sermon aids and Aramaic etymologies, without an organist, without a congregation. So be it. I still have a memory, a soul (let us pray the two not prove at the end of time to be synonymous).

Our text is from the Gospel According to St. John, Chapter 8, verse 11: *Neither do I condemn thee.*

These words are spoken, you will remember, by Jesus to the woman taken in adultery—taken "in the very act," as the posse of Pharisees rather juicily puts it—after none of her accusers has accepted His invitation to cast the first stone. What a beautiful, strange incident this is! Inserted into the narrative, scholars assure us, at a late date, and in a style distinctly unJohannine; and indeed in some manuscripts attached to the second chapter of Luke—a piece of early Christian tradition fluttering hither and thither to find its perch within the canon. As is, the story appears only courtesy of John, the youngest, and least practical, of the Evangelists.

Here, with a gesture unparalleled in the accounts of His life on Earth, Jesus, beset by the brazen importunities of the scribes and Pharisees, stooped down and "with His finger wrote on the ground, as though He heard them not." Nowhere else are we told of His writing. What words He wrote, we are not told, which I take to authenticate the gesture, rather than cast doubt upon it; for why include it, but that it did occur? He wrote idly, irritating His vengeful questioners, and imparting to us yet another impression of our Lord's superb freedom, of the something indolent and abstracted about His earthly career.

Then, the Pharisees dispersed by His magnificent "dare," we read that He rose up, and "saw none but the woman." And He asks her, "Woman, where are those thine accusers?" They are fled. And His aloneness with her reminds us of the later moment when Mary Magdalene, having come to the tomb, and finding only two angels, turns back, and sees Jesus standing, and mistakes Him for the gardener. "Woman, why weepest thou?" He asks her, "Who seekest thou?" and He asks the adulterous woman, "Woman, where are those thine accusers?" and of

His own mother, at the age of twelve, when she rebukes Him for deserting her to discourse with the doctors in the temple, He asks, "How is it that ye sought me?"

How many women, indeed, move through these sacred pages seeking Jesus, and with what sublime delicacy and firmness does He deal with them—His mother Mary and the prophetess Anna, and Joanna and Susanna, and Jairus's daughter and Peter's wife's mother, and the woman who touches His gown so that He knows without looking that virtue has gone out of Him, and the woman of many sins who washes His feet with tears and is forgiven because, though she sinned much, also she loved much; and above all Mary and Martha, who receive Him in their home, and anoint His feet with ointment of spikenard, and are rebuked by Judas, and whose brother Lazarus is raised from the dead, though, in Martha's homely warning, "Lord, by this time he stinketh"!

How homely, indeed, how domestic, is this epic of the New Testament! It sings of private hearths and intimate sorrows, not of palaces and battlefields. The underside and periphery of empire serve as stage for this mightiest and most germane of dramas. Each home a temple: what has our Protestant revolution promulgated but this, this truth spelled plain in the houses and days of the Gospel narrative? How crucial, then, to our present happiness are Christ's pronouncements upon those flanking menaces to the fortress of the household—adultery and divorce.

Jesus preached, scholarship tells us, in a time of cosmopolitan laxity in sexual morals. The Jew, indeed, ever had this fault—in contrast to the rigorous fetishist—of a certain humanistic tolerance. Though Leviticus and Deuteronomy excellently specify death for those who break the Seventh Commandment, the great Hebraic scholar John Lightfoot, in his masterwork, *Horae Hebraicae et Talmudicae,* was unable to locate a single instance of the punishment being carried out. Rather, we are told of a bondmaid who, lying with her master, was scourged and not put to death, "because she was not free." Bathsheba, though she betrayed Uriah in adultery with David, became the Queen of Israel and the mother of Solomon. Eve, seduced by the serpent, yet was the mother of mankind. Gomer, the whorish wife of Hosea, is given to him to be loved, in paradigm of the Lord's continuing love of faithless Israel. And in the new dispensation: Joseph, confronted with swelling evidence of Mary's infidelity, found himself not even willing to make her a public example, and mildly was "minded to put her away privily." Of the two adulterous women Christ encounters in the Gospels, as we have seen, one is commended, and the other is not condemned. Indeed this latter woman was brought to Him, we may conjecture, by the Pharisees to trap Him into asking enforcement of a death penalty universally acknowledged to be absurd. For, as He repeatedly asserts, this is an "adulterous generation." So Jeremiah had found his generation, and Hosea his; for Israel ever breaks its covenant with the Lord, and yet the Lord ever loves, and ever forgives.

Adultery, my friends, is our inherent condition: "Ye have heard that it was said by them of old time, Thou shalt not commit adultery: But I say unto you, That whosoever looketh on a woman to lust after her hath committed adultery with her already in his heart."

But who that has eyes to see cannot so lust? Was not the First Divine Commandment received by human ears, "Be fruitful, and multiply"? Adultery is not a choice to be avoided; it is a circumstance to be embraced. Thus I construe these texts.

But if, dearly beloved, we find our Master abrasively liberal upon the matter of adultery, we find Him even less comfortably stringent upon the matter of divorce. The Pharisaical law of His time was well advanced toward the accommodation of the institution of marriage to the plastic human reality which is never far, I fear, from the heart of Judaism. Bills of divorcement, as described in Deuteronomy 24, might be written when the wife had ceased to find favor in the husband's eyes, "because of some uncleanness in her." Nor did it stop there. A contemporary of the living Jesus, one Rabbi Hillel, propounded that a man might divorce his wife if "she cook her husband's food too much"; and a follower of Hillel, one Rabbi Akiba, offered, with a purity by whose lights our present divorce laws are seen as the hypocritic shambles they are, that he might properly divorce her "if he sees a woman fairer than she."

What does Jesus say to such precepts? That they have been composed in "hardness of heart." That what "God hath joined together, let not man put asunder." That "Whosoever shall put away his wife, and marry another, committeth adultery against her." I quote, from memory, from Mark, the primal Gospel, where the words of our Saviour are least diluted by later incursions of Semitic reasonableness and Greek sophistry. Paul, in Ephesians 5, manfully attempted to mysticize this admittedly "great mystery," claiming of the married couple that "they two shall be one flesh," and substituting, as cosmological analogy, for the covenant between the Lord and Israel the union of Christ and the Church. He writes, "So ought men to love their wives as their own bodies." But most men dislike their own bodies, and correctly. For what is the body but a swamp in which the spirit drowns? And what is marriage, that supposedly seamless circle, but a deep well up out of which the man and woman stare at the impossible sun, the distant bright disc, of freedom?

Let us turn from Holy Writ to the world that surrounds us. Wherein does the modern American man recover his sense of worth, not as dogged breadwinner and economic integer, but as romantic minister and phallic knight, as personage, embodiment, and hero? In adultery. And wherein does the American woman, coded into mindlessness by household slavery and the stupefying companionship of greedy infants, recover her powers of decision, of daring, of discrimination—her dignity, in short? In adultery. The adulterous man and woman arrive at the place of their tryst stripped of all the false uniforms society has assigned them; they come on no recommendation but their own, possess no credentials but those God has bestowed, that is, insatiable egos and workable genitals. They meet in love, for love, with love; they tremble in a glory that is unpolluted by the wisdom of this world; they are, truly, children of light. Those of you—you whose faces stare mutely up at me as I writhe within this imaginary pulpit—those of you who have shaken off your sleep and committed adultery, will in your hearts acknowledge the truth of my characterization.

The Word is ever a scandal. Do not, I beg you, reflexively spurn the interpretation which my meditation upon these portions of Scripture has urged to my understanding.

Verily, the sacrament of marriage, as instituted in its adamant impossibility by our Saviour, exists but as a precondition for the sacrament of adultery. To the one we bring token reverence, and wooden vows; to the other a vivid reverence bred upon the carnal presence of the forbidden, and vows that rend our hearts as we stammer them. The sheets of the marriage bed are interwoven with the leaden threads of eternity; the cloth of the adulterous couch with the glowing, living filaments of transience, of time itself, our element, our only element, which Christ consecrated by entering history, rather than escaping it, as did Buddha.

Why else, I ask you, did Jesus institute marriage as an eternal hell but to spawn, for each sublimely defiant couple, a galaxy of little paradises? Why so conspicuously forgive the adulterous but to lend the force of covert blessing to the apparent imprecation of "adulterous generation." We *are* an adulterous generation; let us rejoice.

For the ministry of Jesus, the forty months of wandering between His baptism and His crucifixion, are not a supplement to, or an abridgment of, the Law. The Law, under a hundred forms, for a thousand tribes, has always existed, and everywhere more or less satisfactorily promotes social order, which is to say, the order of Caesar. But our Lord came not to serve Caesar, or even, as His contemporary kidnappers would have it, to overthrow Caesar; He came, in His own metaphor, not to debase the coinage current, but to put a totally new currency into circulation. Before Him, reality was monochromatic: its image is the slab, the monolith, the monotonous pasture. After Him, truth is dual, alternating, riddled: its image is the chessboard, tilled fields, Byzantine tessellation, Romanesque zigzag,

Siennese striping, and the medieval fool's motley. Christ stands in another light, and His magnificent blitheness, His scorn of all the self-protecting contracts that bind men to the earth, is the shadow of another sun, a shadow brighter than worldly light; by contrast our sunshine burns at His feet blacker than tar.

Amen.

May the peace which passeth all understanding, etc.

7

We look alike, my wife and I. That is what people meeting us for the first time say, sometimes with evident amusement. We do not, ourselves, feel this; nor, during our courtship, was it anything but our differences that intrigued us. She was serenity and beauty; I, agitation and energy. She was moderate, I extreme. She was liberal and ethical and soft, I Barthian and rather hard. Above all, she was female and fruitful, and I masculine and hungry. My impulse, to *eat* her, to taste, devour, and assimilate, which continues into even this our misery, though my bite has become murderous, began with the first glimpse; she was standing, in pleated tennis garb, in the windy warmth of an April day when tennis had become suddenly possible, beneath a blooming fruit tree, a small apple or a crabapple. Within this dappled shade, her head grazing the petalled limbs, the lowest was so low, Jane's prettily pallid form appeared one with her arbor. There was a piquance in her seeking this delicate shelter, on so delicately bright a day; I later learned she was allergic to the sun.

Both pale, both moderately above median height, both blue-eyed and not a bit fat, tendony rather, with the something tense about us qualified by an aura indifferent and ashen as of stalks of smoke, we make, in public, a twinned impression intensified, of course, by two decades' worth of phrase-swapping, signal-giving, and unconscious facial aping. We have been worn by the same forces into parallel spindles. We lie down in bed together side by side and turn as if on a single lathe. We resort, I sense, to a common expression under stress—an upward tilting of the head and tighter trimming of the mouth that lets our besieger know we have withdrawn into a fastidious and, despite ourselves, shared privacy.

Oh I know, I know, dear unknown reader, that just thinking of this woman tricks my prose into a new ease of fancy and airiness of cadence; I am home. But do not be fooled; this ease and comfort are not palliation, they are the disease.

The Doctor Reverend Wesley Augustus Chillingworth, Jane's father, performed as professor of ethics at the divinity school I attended. A green slanting campus, a lake at the bottom, a great ironstone chapel erected by some industrial (industrious: in dust try us) sinner at the top. A rangy town beyond, with bars and buses for its denizens, while for us there was a screen of elms and ells, and bells, bells pealing the hour, the half-hour, the quarter, until the air seemed permanently liquefied, and spilling everywhere like mercury. Chillingworth was a short, square man whose docile sallow squareness made him seem shorter than he was; he delivered his dry lectures in a virtual whisper, often facing the blackboard or an antique brown globe of the heavens left in his room from an era when natural science and theology were, if not lovers, flirts. The orgy of reading that must have consumed his youth and prime had left him, in his late fifties, wearing a great rake's faintly cocky air of exhaustion; there was a twinkle in his dryness as he led us through the desiccated debates of the Greeks, of the hedonists and the Platonists, the Peripatetics and the Cyrenaics, the Stoics and the Epicureans, over the one immense question, *Is the pleasant the good, or not quite?* His course epitomized everything I hated about academic religion; its safe and complacent faithlessness, its empty difficulty, its transformation of the tombstones of the passionate dead into a set of hurdles for the living to leap on their way to an underpaid antique profession. The old scholar's muttering manner seemed to acknowledge this, as without mercy he dragged us, his pack of pimply postulates, from Hottentot tabus and Eskimo hospitality (fuck my wife, you blubber) on to the tedious Greeks and the neo-Platonists (how can the soul be a form? how can it not be? how can God be a self? what else can He be? what is the good, then, but absorption into God? what is the good *of* it?) and further on to the rollicking saints, knitting their all-weather space-suits of invisible wool, Augustine and his *concupiscentia,* Bonaventura and his *gratia,* Anselm and his *librum arbitrium,* Aquinas and his *synderesis,* Duns Scotus and his *pondus naturae,* Occam and his razor, and Heaven knows who all else. By spring we had won through to Grotius and his *jus gentium,* and as modern ethics unfolded under Chillingworth's muttering I had the parallel pleasure, as it were in running footnote, of seducing his daughter. We met in the cool British sunshine of Hobbesian realism, hit balls at each other with unbridled egoism, and agreed to play again, as partners. By the time of our next date, Hume was exploding "ought" and "right" and Bentham was attempting to reconstruct hedonism with maximization formulas. Our first kiss came during Spinoza, more *titillatio* than *hilaritas.* Yet I felt my *conatus,* sombre center of my self, beautifully lift from my diaphragm as, in the darkness of my shut lids, her gravity for the first time impinged on mine. As Kant attempted to soften rationalism with categorical imperatives and *Achtung,* Jane let me caress her breast through her sweater. By the time of Hegel's monstrous identification of morality with the demands of the state, my hand was hot in her bra, and my access had been universalized to include her thighs. How solid and smooth this pedant's daughter was! I had expected her to be spun of cobwebs. We were both twenty-two and virgins. The weather loosened; the nights were warm. Schopenhauer exalted will and Nietzsche glorified brutality, cunning, rape, and war. All earlier ethics stood exposed as "slave virtues" and "herd virtues." Jane, in her room atop the great dusty vault of stacked books and learned journals her father called his "study," let me undress her—no, to be honest, undressed herself, with a certain graceful impatience, I having made of her clothing an asymmetric mess of rumples and undone snaps. She flicked away the last morsel of underwear and tucked her hands behind her head in the pose of a napping picnicker and let me look. This was not my first naked female. You will remember the redhead deftly evoked pages ago, and there was a bony fellow-counsellor one summer we may never find the space for. But Jane was as to these as the cut marble is to the melted wax of the preliminary models. No formula, utilitarian or idealist, could quite do justice to the living absoluteness of it. Here was a fact, five foot seven inches long, and of circumferences varying with infinite subtlety from ankles to hips, from waist to skull. The window was open, admitting evening air and light enough to marvel by. Bands of green and salmon glowed behind the spired horizon. Her girlhood room (childish wallpaper of a medallioned cottage alternate with a woolly shepherd, back turned, standing among dogs, and tacked over with collegiate prints of Klee, Miró, and Cézanne) surrounded me like a fog of dream furniture as my eyes in twilight drank. Her father cleared his throat below. Jane made silent offer of a laugh and removed her hands from behind her head; she pulled me down into herself to snuff out my staring. "It's meant to be natural," she whispered, her first reproof, if reproof it was, or the first I remember, the first that shamed me, and that has remained preserved, beetle in amber, in my exuded sense of having—in having taken such awed delight in the sight of her (*Achtung,* indeed)—done something wrong. The British idealists, Green and Bradley, attempted to lift the human self, timeless and unitary, away from the ravening reach of analytical science. Do not think, because we became naked together, we made love. This was the Fifties. There were complications both technical and spiritual, traditional and existential. While Pierce, James, and Dewey, with native American makeshift wit, tried to reverse the divine current and wag the transcendental Dog with the tail of credulity's practical benefits, Jane proved alarmingly adept at dry-fucking (forgive this term among others, Ms. Prynne and whatever vestrymen are in attendance; that which has existence [*ens*] must have a name [*nomen*]). Alarming because her adeptness showed she had done it before. Kneeling or lying sideways, her hands no-nonsensically placed on my buttocks for alignment's and pressure's sake, she would fricate our scratchy contact until one of us, as often she before me as I before her, would trip and come. The laggard would follow suit. What poetry in virginity!—Jane's little gasp at my shoulder, and her glans-crushing push, and the leaps within her unseen, and the wet revelation of my semen, glutinous in her pussy or glistening on her belly like an iota of lunar spit. Penetrant love by comparison comes muffled. The existentialists, beginning with Kierkegaard, who set up a clever roar less unlike Nietzsche's than the tender-minded would wish, did away with essence and connection and left us with an "authenticity" whose relativity is unconfessed. Jane was slow to say she loved me. Of her virginity (a mere wet inch away) she said she should "save herself." For some other? As the logical positivists thought to end human confusion by careful reference to the dictionary (see C. L. Stevenson, *Ethics and Language,* 1944, and the final text Chillingworth assigned), I introduced the word "marriage." Jane nodded, silently. I saw her as "wife"* and went blind with pride.

To what extent, you may well ask, did I seduce this good stately girl as an undermining and refutation of the old polymath's theology, his wry dimness worse than Deism, in which I recognized, carried

* The word, by the way, is just the Anglo-Saxon *wīf,* for "woman." My wife, *ma femme,* this cunt indentured to me. Sad to say, lib-lubbers.

some steps further by a better mind, my father's terrifying bumbling at the liberal Lord's busywork? Chillingworth would dustily cough beneath us at the oddest moments, so often in synchrony with orgasm as to suggest telepathic discomfort. I was slaying him that the Lord might live.

On his side, I believe, there was nothing so fanciful. He lived in this world. He knew that girls mature and their pelves become butterfly nets for the capture of chromosomes. Jane was the second of three daughters. The first was married, divorced, and crazy—so crazy that, in those years, she opposed Truman's intervention in Korea, and spoke of his dropping the atomic bomb as an atrocity. The younger daughter was chipping away at geology at the University of Colorado. Jane had graduated from Oberlin and had returned home for lack of a better offer; she worked mornings in a local nursery school, and taught Sunday school as well. She played the piano and the flute. She read Victorian novels. But for me, her beaux were older men (an affectedly weedy assistant prof in comp. rel. with extensive nostril-hairs and caustically bad breath from pipe-smoking; a tiny ex-Jesuit with ursine brown eyes and a clangorous stammer to match the manacle of his handshake; a plump pacifist curate with one of the pioneer beards of the fuzzily forming revolution) or members of an accredited minority, a Nigerian here, a Korean there, all of them on the make, ministerially speaking. Jane attracted suitors she could easily shed. Old Chillingworth may even have been pleased when I, with my burrish manners, appeared; my grade in his course had been B+, and my supernatural politics amused him.

"What is it," he would ask me in those not entirely stilted parlor interviews before I would ascend with Jane to the hypothetical study-hall of her room or else take her out to the surrogate paradise of a Chinese meal and a Bogart movie, "that you find so heartening in Barth? Wherein lies this specificity that pleases you?"

And my core of conviction, under his temperate gray-domed gaze, exploded like an overheated Ping-Pong ball.

"You know," he would add, tapping his pipe or a fork or his fountain pen on an ashtray or a plate or the edge of a book, "this type of radical Paulinism is a recurrent strain in the church. Marcion. Bonaventura. Duns Scotus. Occam. Flacius."

I couldn't argue. I didn't want to. I didn't know enough. I liked him. Or do I repeat myself?

Oh, and Jane herself in those years. So charming, patient, calm, abstracted, fearless, healthy, but for her solar allergy. As she walked down a cloistered path toward me it was as if a lone white rose were arriving by telegraph.

Do I regret marrying her? No more can I regret having been born. The question is, having been born, what now?

The answer being, in this place, shave, and go to the bar. Bliss! The afternoon opens before me wide as a fairway split by a straight drive. Graham Greene is right. Gratitude is the way He gets us, when we have gnawed off a leg to escape His other snares.

8

Two decades later, Jane has little changed. Two childbearings and a miscarriage and an aeon of standing at the parsonage sink have put a pucker here and a popped vein there, but her way of walking is unchanged, her arms still swing in her strange, conceited, absent-minded way, as if with every stride she is burnishing herself brighter still.

In the middle of the golf course, this reminds me, yesterday, in mid-6-iron (I hit it fat and it found a bunker; the sand out here is reprocessed glass), my tireless subconscious flashed on my self-portrait as I so studiously examined Jane naked on her bed and I recognized my pose as that of a housewife bending over a long porcelain sink where a single Brillo pad has been left lying, unmoistened, expectant, abrasive, symbolic of weary worlds of work to come.

This is going to be one of those thick-fingered days. A little fray in the typewriter ribbon moves back and forth like a sentry. A spattering of rain last night, so heavy and sudden I assumed the air-conditioner had gone haywire, has left a legacy of puffy clouds whose occasional shadow, like the shadow of a passing sentry (they guard me on all sides), activates the air of this room ominously.

Jane, two decades later, though the intonation of her person and that of mine have come to be mutual echoes, and the dimple in her cheek has impressed a brother into the center of my chin, and the original russet of my hair and the chestnut of hers have thinned and faded to an interchangeable what's-the-use brown, with gray added to your taste (she is not bald on top, like me, but her forehead has heightened, and when she pulls and flattens her hair back in front of a mirror, something she is inexplicably fond of doing, she looks, as she says, "skinned"), does, by another light—the light, say, of a fireplace as she stirs a Martini with her finger and gazes into the glow, or of the bedroom 60-watt as she darts, headfirst, into her nightie—appear *totaliter aliter*, an Other, a woman, and, as such, marketable. I did seriously hope, amid the pressure-warped improbabilities of my affair with Alicia, to mate Jane with Ned Bork, and thus arrange a happy ending for all but the Pharisees.

For one thing, he was not all that young. He had been in some business—peddling real estate, or making fancy ceramics, or partly managing a ski resort in some Yankee state; or perhaps he ran a pottery shop in a ski lodge that was for sale—before getting the "call," and undergoing, at his family's wise indulgence, divinity school. He was thirty at least.

For another, he reminded me of those thirty-year-olds who had been courting Jane before I carried her off. Ned had the beard of the pacifist, the modest stature and sexual ambiguity of the Jesuit, the pipe and affected drawl of the assistant prof. I always felt I had, in removing Jane from her circle of harmless seminarian misfits, deflected her from her destiny. Here was her chance to reclaim it, to wake from the numb nightmare of marriage to me. I did not, even in my lovelorn madness, imagine that she and Ned would marry; but perhaps they would clasp long enough to permit me to slip out the door with only one bulky armload of guilt.

For a third, they liked each other. They had the same milky human kindness, the same preposterous view of the church as an adjunct of religious studies and social service, the same infuriating politics, a warmed-over McGovernism of smug lamenting: never did they think to see themselves, however heavily their heads nodded, as two luxurious blooms on a stalk fibrous with capital and cops. Of course Jane must have felt in Ned her suitors returned to her; and he, my reasoning was, must see in her a female who, unlike whatever insatiable opposite numbers had scared him away from marriage, would have the grace and wisdom to let the appearance of submission be hers. My acquaintance with the girls of Ned's generation was (at this point) purely scholastic, but I read often enough in the fidasustenative newsletters and quarterlies that pour through a minister's letter slot like urine from a cow's vulva that they (these girls), deprived of shame and given the pill, had created a generation of impotent lads the like of which had not been seen since nannies stopped slicing off masturbators' thumbs. Impotent, I must say, I was (then) never: as ready to stand and ejaculate as to stand and spout the Apostles' Creed. This cause for rejoicing turned out to be, when in the phosphorescent decay of all we held dear old grudges began to twinkle, one of Jane's complaints; if I had not been, her case argued, so eternally upright, she might out of compassion have mastered a dozen lewd tricks and excited herself to a flutter of multiple orgasms in the bargain. So Bork's supposed semipotence became an asset, an added pastel of probability as, on the hectic sketchpad of wishful thinking, I embowered the twain, a silken and limp Adonis and his mellowed, maternal Venus, the blasphemous and opulent couple goaded by remorse toward me (me, the invisible presiding blasphemed, the mutually loved and detested, the *y* of the triune equation) into one extravagance of penetration after another.

Fuck my wife, you blubber.

Many the night did Bork come for dinner and

stay, while I plodded out into the sleet in placation of the telephone, to minister unto a comatose matrix of tubes and medicines that had once been a parishioner or (not often; we were no bolder than we needed to be) to visit Alicia in her airy tract house. Many the night did I return and find them, my mate and my curate, still propped in a daze at the table, or bedded in opposing easy chairs by the fireplace, noogling away at the brandy and beer (they both had the capacities of vats, another auspicious affinity) and gently fumbling for (as far as I could tell) the pacifier of a social cure-all in the tumbled blankets of their minds. What babies they were! I thought they might at least fornicate out of conversational boredom. But they never seemed to weary of talking. My nostrils stuffed with the musky stench of death or sex, my shoulders hoary with sleet and woe, I looked down upon them like an impatient God who, by some crimp in His contract with Noah, cannot destroy. I say "sleet"; it must have been winter. For more seasons than I can correlate the weather of, my prayers that I be betrayed ascended in vain. I prayed, and cried, and tried. I tried the nudge direct:

(In bed, with Mrs. Marshfield and her reek of Cognac) "Do you find Ned sexually attractive?"

"I like his philosophy."

"And his acne?" (constantly at cross-purposes with myself, could bite my tongue)

"I don't mind it."

"What do you think he does, for romance?"

"I have no idea. We never discuss such things. Could I please go to sleep? The whole room is spinning around and I might throw up."

(Not to be dissuaded; the hound of Heaven) "Why *don't* you discuss such things? I'd think you would. Isn't it a little abnormal, that you don't?"

"Tom, there's a whole other world to discuss, besides ego gratification."

"Am I talking about ego gratification?" (she had her father's gift, of enlightening me when I least wanted it)

"That's all you ever talk about, lately."

"You detect a change in me, lately?" (Come on, guess. Alicia's ass sits on my head like an aureole, look. *Guess.* Do *some*thing to get me out of this.)

"Not really. You seem a little less frantic."

"In what sense frantic? When was I ever frantic?" (Me, me, what do you make of me, Mimi?)

"*Please* stop thrashing around. I really might be sick. I wish you wouldn't keep leaving me and Ned alone all the time, it makes us so nervous we both drink too much."

"There's something very beautiful about Ned, don't you think? He doesn't have any of our generation's hang-ups."

"He has hang-ups of his own," mumbled this maddening bed-partner, this flesh of my flesh.

"Oh? Does he leave you kind of titillated but unsatisfied? Want to make love, just to relieve the tension?"

"Isn't tomorrow Sunday?"

"Better yet, *today* is Sunday. Roll over and tell me about Ned's hang-ups."

A soft snore signals her conquest of liquor, lust, marital heckling, and time. She is beautiful in oblivion. I envy her. She has the style of Grace if not its content. Her goodness keeps defeating me. My hate of her, my love of her, meet at the bottom of our rainbow, a circle.

And the nudge indirect:

"How does Jane seem to you?" Walking Ned home, through the parsonage yard, I take his plump upper arm for steadiness' sake.

"Pleasant, as always. *Très engagée.*" He disengages his arm. Drunkenness doesn't make him unsteady; it merely exaggerates his boarding-school mannerisms.

"Her engagingness doesn't strike you as a cover-up?"

"Not frightfully, really." He senses stressful depths, and has borrowed from me the odious trick of clowning in the face of mystery. "What," he asks, "exactly does my reverend superior mean?"

"Well, I don't know." And I don't. A natural agnostic, converted to right-handedness by a Little League father. "I worry about Jane." This is true. "She's not happy." Is this true? Has she ever been happy since her father stopped clearing his throat under her body? "Not"—I plunge—"ful*filled,* if you can stand the term."

"Here I stand, I can do no other" (drunker than I had thought, and sillier: what callow punks the seminaries are sending us, since the frontier dried up).

I offered him a lesson in practical religion. "Being a minister's wife is curiously isolating, you're always being nice to people as a formality, you forget to *feel*. Now that the boys are breaking away, the only person Jane seems to enjoy talking to is *you.*"

"And you, surely."

(Laugh, as memorably bitter as I can make it; etching with acid) "Don't kid. It must be obvious to you, how little she and I communicate."

"Not so. Not obvious. Would never have supposed that to be the case. You even look like one another." He stands at his front door, teetering a touch. Streetlight strikes a gleam from his glassy eyes. His beard makes his face hard to read. The mouth a mere hole, with a sinister drawgate of teeth. Santa Claus as heroin pusher. Even his ears, if they showed, might be a clue to his heart. His centrally parted hair is enough like a woman's to tip my insides toward kissing him good-night. I teeter also. I tug back the abhorrent impulse and yank its leash savagely. All outward composure, I continue (the nudge semi-direct):

"Well I'm very grateful, for your being so sympathetic to Jane. She's in a strange time of her life and needs someone not me she can talk to. You seem to be it."

"My pleasure," quoth he: this speckle-browed dutiful prep-school prick (there must a better term, Ms. Prynne, but I'm word-weary, my stint is up, the bawdy hand of the dial is now upon the prick of noon).

Mock not my revelations. They are the poor efforts of a decent man to mitigate an indecent bind, an indecently airtight puzzle. Been reading a lot of John Dickson Carr—his many locked rooms. Idea for a funny sermon (funny idea for a sermon?): The Case of the Empty Tomb, solved by an eccentric fat detective, fat, gruff, uncanny, cleanliness-obsessed Ponto Pilato. Who, really, *were* those two "angels"? *Why* did Mary mistake Him for a gardener? Was there a "second Osworld"? Et cet. This room feels pretty airless itself. Those clouds striding the wall. The air-conditioner like the muzzle of a final solution. Get me out of this, as Dutch Schultz (or was it Molly Bloom, or Psalm 22?) said. Anyway, probably already been done, in one of the Dead Sea Scrolls, by Andman Willsin.

I hate this day's pages. The depression grows fangs, this second week.

9

More dialogue, it aërates Hell.

Alicia: "What time *is* it?"

Me: "Time for me to go."

"Couldn't your meeting go on a half-hour longer?"

"Not likely. It's not a meeting. In theory I'm at the hospital, and in fact there *is* one call I must make."

"What would you have been, if you hadn't been a minister?"

"A gigolo? A prison warden? A private detective?" I am dressing, so the answers are preoccupied. The first is immodest, the second is self-rebuke, the third an honest boyhood ambition. "Why do you ask?"

The plump body, enjoyed and dismissed, sits up on the bed, expressing indignation. How frontal she is!—her breasts, her shining knees, her broad mouth and wideset, rubbed-looking, half-blind eyes. "Just wondering if you still think it's your thing."

"Because I keep fucking you? And being a hypocrite?"

"I don't mind the hypocrisy, it's your unhappiness."

"What else can I do?" Than be a minister. Than deceive Jane and keep my appointments. Than be unhappy—I resented, really, being told I was. "Freud speaks," I said, "of normal human unhappiness. Pascal says man's glory is that he knows his misery. I feel pretty good, actually."

"You always feel good," Alicia told me, "when you're with me."

Not precisely true; her saying this engendered queasiness.

But true enough to let it by. Dressed, I kissed her; my clothes were armor against her nakedness. She lifted up onto her knees, the mattress heaving in sympathy, and pressed her body against mine, which had to move a step closer the bed, lest she topple forward. Careful, don't cry, moisture is telltale, and the smell of flesh carries. "It *is* odd," I said, with a bow to Professor Chillingworth, deceased, "that feeling good and being good don't seem to be the same thing."

She snuffled warmly into my dickey. "Are you sure?"

"You want me to leave Jane and the ministry?

It'd have to be both. And my children. And my lifetime subscription to *Tidbits for Pulpit Use*."

She laughed through her tears, snorting; I feared a sudden extrusion of phlegm, and backed her face from my chest. Alicia looked up. "Is it so impossible?" she asked and, attempting to study my face an angel's wingbeat longer, answered, "It is." Her spectacles sat brittle on the bedside table; I felt her considering reaching and putting them on, to see me better, and deciding instead to give my waist a tighter squeeze.

I had to counterattack or surrender. "Why do you want me," I asked, "that way? You have me this way."

"I could have anybody this way."

"Then do. Do. You've had lots of others—your musical types, who knows who else, the playground instructor, the man in the oil truck, go ahead."

"O.K., I will," said Alicia, sniffing and licking my belt.

"What would I do, outside the ministry? It's my life. It's my afterlife."

"Be a gigolo or a private detective. Just stop being your own prisoner."

"I'm working on it," I said. "Mostly at night. I can't sleep."

"That's something," she conceded, dropping her arms to release me now.

Now *I* could not quite let go; she was an adhesive complex of interlocking slacknesses and fulcrums, just fucked, in the bald late light of her slanting room, upon the rumpled sunburst of her quilt, whose pattern when we had drunk enough wine I would see as cascading organ notes. "It's hard," I told her.

"It is," she said, soft center of my new world.

To Jane I said, "Have you ever wanted to have an affair?"

We were in bed, her back was to me. "You assume I never have."

"I guess I do."

"Why is that?"

"Because you're a minister's wife."

"What brings this on, anyway?"

"Oh, nothing. Middle age. Angst. It occurs to me I've never really thought enough about you. What *you* want. What *you* feel. Whatever happened to all those boy friends of yours?"

"I didn't have that many."

"Well, you knew how anatomy worked, before I showed up."

"It was just instinct, Tom. Don't be so jealous."

"I am a jealous God. I covet my neighbor's wife's ass."

"Which neighbor? Not that neurotic Harlow woman."

"I love her veils." When I looked down upon Mrs. Harlow in the third pew seat she always took, I thought of beekeepers, purdah, and mourning.

However ultramontane my theology strikes you (silent veiled reader out there), in liturgy I lazily gravitate toward low; though I like myself in drag, church is not a costume ball. Jane seemed about to drift into sleep with all my precious questions in her pockets. "Well, have you?"

"Have I what?"

"Wanted other men?"

"Oh, I guess."

"You guess."

"It's too silly to talk about. Sure, in some other world it'd be fun to go to bed with everybody and see what it's like."

"In some other world. I'm touched by your supernaturalism." It was true I was. "Well, who would you begin with? Of the men we know."

"You?"

"Come on. You know I don't satisfy you." I have always admired, in the dialogues of Plato, Socrates' smoothness in attaining his auditors' consent to his premises.

Jane said, "I know no such thing. Are you projecting, or agitating, or what?"

"An ecumenical mixture?" I offered. "Tell me about men. Whatever happened to that pacifist? How do you feel about Ned Bork?"

"He's awfully young."

"All the more vigorous for that. And endlessly sympathetic, don't you find? Don't you love his brand of Jesus? The poor ye have with you not necessarily always. I come to bring not peace but a peace demonstration."

"That is nice."

The gravity of her warm mass pulled me away from Ned. Her phrase, "fun to go to bed with everybody," had packed her with a delectable, permeable substance, many tiny little possible bodies. As I struggled to roll her over, Jane said, sociologically, "It's so un*fair*, women spend their days doing physical work, while men like you who sit at desks or worry about people wind up at night with all this undischarged energy."

"Ah," I said, "but you have two *x* chromosomes, to my one."

To Ned I said, "That sermon went rather far, I thought."

"How so, sir?" Threatened, he tilted back his head, so his lips showed through his beard, pink and ladylike.

"Do you really believe," I asked him, "that an oligarchy of blacks and chicanos and college dropouts would come up with a better system, quote unquote, than the corporation board of Exxon?"

"I wouldn't mind seeing it tried. It can't be worse."

"That's where you flower people, in my needless to say humble view, are wrong. It could be a lot worse. Has been, and will be, I expect."

"Does this expectation, in your view, excuse the

church from any present proclamation upon the relative improvability of the world?"

"Does this improvability, in *your* view, excuse the church from its task to minister to the world as it finds it? More immediately, does your perception of the businessman in our congregation as an agent of an evil system prevent you from ministering to his immortal soul?"

"Christ said, It is easier for the camel, and so on."

"He also said, Judge not, and so on. Let us sentimentalize neither the rich nor the poor. If their assets were reversed, they would act like one another. The material world, viewed spiritually, is a random grid. Wherever we are placed within it, our task is to witness, to offer a way out of the crush of matter and time. You have been placed here, under me. I wish to hear no more New Left sloganizing from my pulpit."

Ned began, "Simple compassion—"

"Compassion is *not* simple. That is where you so heretically condescend. You give your simple compassion to those you imagine to be simple. Love thy *neighbor*. Love what is near, not what is far. Love the rich, the well off, the white; love the poor suburban burgher who drags in here because he dimly senses another feeble ally in his perilous battle to keep from thieves what other thieves have won for him. If this society strikes you as criminal, remember the criminal on the cross. Forget for a moment this Moloch of social change, and pray to the true God, the God above change, the God who destroyed Rome and Christendom, the God who jealously reserves to His own kingdom the new Jerusalem of perfect equality and justice—pray to Him that, your penitential term with me completed, you may be called to a slum parish, and there sharpen your compassion on another grindstone of circumstance. At all points, Ned, the world presses us toward despair and forgetfulness of God. At no point, perhaps, more than here, in this empty church."

The church was around us. Between the windows stone plaques remembered forgotten pillars; the pipes of the organ played a hugely silent chord. Ned no doubt argued back, there was much to be said on his side; and I responded until weary. My hope was not to convert him, but to alienate him, so he would be eased of guilt, if moved to sleep with my wife.

Mrs. Harlow came to me after a meeting of the Distaff Circle. Without her Sunday veil her face bore the fine reticulations of middle age upon a pretty oval that had not changed since she was seventeen. Her beauty, now fragile, sat upon her nervous as a tremor. And the gray of her eyes had an unsettling purity, as of metal atomized into sky. Some Southern parentage lingered in her accent. Her manner, though unimpeachable, seemed slightly alarmed. She asked, "Reverend Marshfield, do you notice, there seems to be more and more music?"

"Where?"

"In the *ser*vice."

"I hadn't noticed."

"Oh, it's very noticeable out there. I *do* think Mrs. Crick deserves a great deal of credit, she's performed miracles for the children's choir, my Julie wouldn't miss a time now and we used to have to *bribe* her to go. But that anthem by Praetorius I do believe went on for a good seven minutes. Gerry was taking up the collection and stood so long at the back with the plates he said his arm went utterly to sleep."

"You think the music is overpowering the rest?"

"Not if my pastor doesn't. I was raised to care deeply about the Word, but I realize that was a con*sid*erable time ago." Her eyes never appeared to blink; their fine gray kept coming. She stood some inches closer than necessary, like Europeans and the hard-of-hearing.

"No time at all ago," I said. "A thousand ages in his sight—"

"You *do* flatter. My husband also says some of the elderly deacons are disturbed by the guitars."

"Well, Mrs. Crick is trying—"

"Oh, I *know* Mrs. Crick can do no wrong!" And again I had to observe, of a woman flouncing down the aisle, that her bottom was surprisingly expressive; Mrs. Harlow's was slimmer than some, but exquisitely weighted, a scales shifting balance at each nice, righteous stride.

"Alicia, love."

"Yes, lover."

"Are you conscious of being more ambitious, in the service, than you used to be? How many instrumentalists did that Handel Concerto in F take?"

"Some, but it didn't cost the church anything. They were friends or friends of friends."

"It seemed to me Ned cut his sermon so we wouldn't run long."

"No, he didn't cut it, he planned it short. I told him ahead of time."

"Oh. You two worked it up without telling me."

"Well, if you want to put it that way. Did you mind? Didn't you like the music?"

"I loved it. You have a great touch. I just wonder if the church should become a concert hall."

"Why not? It isn't much else."

"Oh?"

"Except of course a display case for you."

"You feel that, or are you making some other point?"

"You know I feel that, I told you six months ago, before we—were like this." We were in bed. Her hand flicked to indicate our bodies with a certain impatience: her gum-chewing hard self showed. The summer was past. The sky hung dull as pewter in the leafless windows of her bedroom. The oil truck in the alley whined. Her children for much of the summer vacation had been visiting Mr. Crick, who had remarried in Minnesota; they returned from school at 2:30. It was 1:47, stated Alicia's little vanilla-colored bedside electric clock, which had needle-fine, scarcely visible hands, green-tipped for nighttime luminescence, and a chic shy shape, that of a box being squeezed in an invisible press, so its smooth sides bulged. I said, "Time for me to go."

"I suppose," Alicia sighed, and did not cling as I swung my legs from the bed.

I stood and explained, "I told the Distaff Circle I'd help with the hall decorations for the Harvest Supper."

"You don't have to explain."

I put on my underwear snappily and cleared my throat and released what had been on my mind. "From a conversation I had with Mrs. Harlow I got the impression our relationship might not be entirely a thing unseen."

Alicia, propped on a pillow, her small breasts licked by the light, made her wise mouth, looked at me flat as a cat looks at one, and advised, "Screw Mrs. Harlow."

Dear silenced words, your recall makes me fond. Contrary to my preachments to Thaddeus Bork, being far makes these souls, once neighbors of mine, more dear. I hear now, what the roaring of desire and dread in my ears deafened me to at the time, that they each wanted, expected, something from me, from me. In their midst I was powerful. And felt helpless. Here, in this desert routine, I am stripped and anonymous, and feel mighty. The splendor of space and the splendid waste of time enter my self-negation. See Saints, Lives of.

10

I hoped her black car parked at his brown-and-green cottage was an optical illusion. The naked foot I had classified as a favered* hallucination. I had said nothing to her. We were meeting less frequently, in shorter days pinched mean, pinched black and blue, by our busyness of the fall. Fall, fall, who named thee? The year's graceful aping of our cosmic plunge. How much more congenial, in its daily surrender, to our organic hearts than the gaudy effortful comedy, the backwards-projected travesty, of spring. The diver rises feet first from the pool, the splash seals over where he has been, the board receives him on its tip like a toad's tongue snaring a fly. The stone has been rolled away. O carapace-cracking, rib-pulling halleluiahs! The

* Well, what can this mean? I want to be favored, though fevered? Or my fever has the vanilla flavor of the bedside clock just described at such unexpectedly lovesick length?

agony of resurrection, a theme for Unamuno. The agony of dried tubers. See Eliot, Tom. See Tom run. Run, Tom, run.

To work. Our leading character, Tom, miscast as a Protestant clergyman, could not ignore the telltale clue of the black car the second time he saw it. No doubt there were other times when he had not seen it. This time, Tom had been lying awake, listening to noises that a sane man would have dismissed as the normal creak of wood and breathing of somniacs but that he preferred to hear as the step of a murderous intruder, or the half-smothered shuttle of his fate being woven. His wife slept heavily, moaning, *Crucify him, crucify him*. Nixon, of course. Nixema, the noxious salve for liberal sores. O, cursed be the sleep of the just! Barren fig trees, every one. He arose impatiently, went to the window, threw up the sash, and lo! to his wondering eyes did appear . . .

Ignore it. It was just an old black Chevrolet. Sitting a-wink with moonlight and arc light. But, like the cinder of a comet's head, trailing after it a pluming tail of fair skin, gold fuzz, white sheets, undiluted sunshine, radiant intimacy. A tousled pale treasure of flesh and moistened oxygen that had been his. Tom returned to bed but could not sleep. His eyes had sipped poison. Covetousness threatened to burst his skull, ire his spleen, and lust his groin. He twisted, he writhed; the twinned body beside him had ceased to turn on the same lathe. He arose. Learning from frosty experience, and in deference to the Heraclitean river which indeed would be some weeks chiller than when he first stepped into it, for the month had become December and the holy season Advent, he put on not only his pajama bottoms but socks (probably mismatched in the dark, though the odds were shortened by the high percentage of his socks that were black), shoes, an overcoat that had gloves in the pockets, and, from the front hall rack (the slavelike, treacherous stairs negotiated), a little wool hat given him ten years earlier by his then-living mother and which, after years of disuse, the hat bearing too comical a suggestion of a Scots gamewarden or a stage detective, he had taken to wearing again. Mother, protect me. 'Gainst hail and cold and doveshit be thou a shield.

The blue night barked as I opened the door. Down, Fido. An inch of dry snow mottled the brittle lawn. I left tracks. Thinking fast if not well, I did not make straight for the windows baleful with the same mute lamp that had lent substance to the earlier orgy, but held to the brick walk by the parsonage, tripping lightly lest my scuffle stir the Nixonophobe snug above, and left my turf through the gated gap in the hedge provided. Stealthily I approached Ned's house by the pavement, where my steps blended with those of daytime innocents whose hearts had not been pounding like crazy mine. Hark! A far car drew nearer in the ghostly grid of snow-glazed ways. As plain beneath the streetlight as a blot on table linen, I met with no inspiration but to merge with the other blot—that is, to squeeze open the door of Alicia's black Chevrolet, push forward the balky seat, crawl into the back, and crouch on the floor in an attitude that, were I a Moslem and Mecca properly aligned, would have done for prayer.

For minutes I froze there, *motor immotus*. The enveloping aroma of floor mat, haunted by old orange peels and lost M & Ms, was my sufficient universe. At last convinced that my criminal commotion had not alerted the *civitas,* I adjusted my crouch more comfortably, pulled my mothering hat down to my ears, and tried to spare my cheek prolonged acquaintance with the waffly pattern of the rubber mat as it arched across the driveshaft. Sleepiness, long courted, assailed me inconveniently.

At this point an obligation arises (you insatiable ideal reader, you) for an account of my thoughts during my grotesque but somewhat happy vigil. I notice I have slipped into the first person; a Higher Wisdom, it may be, directs my style.

Somewhat happy. I have always been happy, Americanly, in cars. I acquired my license as soon as the law allowed. I became my father's chauffeur. The first piece of furniture I could drive. A car's stale, welded sameness within its purposive speed. Tranquillity in flux. That attic redhead I mentioned (remember?) was undressed and inspected (partially, both) by the submarine glow of a parked car's panel. A generation and the hump of a lifetime later, my dour Dart becomes a hydrofoil skimming above the asphalt waves of the highway of life, severing me from any terrestrial need to be polite, circumspect, wise, reverent, kind, affectionate, entertaining, or instructive. Encapsulation in any form short of the coffin has a charm for me: the cave of wicker porch furniture that children arrange, the journey of a letter from box to sack to sack to slot, the astronaut's fatalistic submission to a web of formulae computers have spun. My position crouched on the floor was in a sense chosen; chances of discovery would only be slightly improved by lying on the rear seat. But being down, empathizing my way along the floor mat's edge, through the crumby detritus of the Crick children's snacks, past a button and chewed pencil stub, into the nether region of the driver's seat, where a square foot of fluff and stray licorice and the red pull-bands of cigarette packs cozily defied purgation and a system of rusty springs inscrutably impinged upon strips of gray felt, pleased me, yea, pleased me not only in its concentrated pose of humiliation but in its potential of springing up, like a child at a surprise party, and startling Alicia into loving laughter.

In fact, after what was a long twenty minutes or a short eternity, my aching back and waffled knees compelled me to sit on the seat, slumped over to avoid decapitation by passing headlight beams.

Were the lovers asleep? Was Jane not? I had vowed to return to the parsonage, my boiling rage chilled to a permissive slush, when the light above Ned's door came on. From the sliver of him that for an instant showed he seemed to be wearing a tangled shirt and an unbuttoned beard. Alicia had donned, or redonned, her red dress, in the Christmas spirit, and in her warmed condition hadn't bothered to zip her loden coat. Jaunty, brisk, her car key pre-fished from her purse and ready as a stiletto in her gloved hand, she crossed to her car, my cave, and opened the door. Though I was slumped so the ashy stench of the sidearm ashtray crowded my nostrils, a beam of radiance from Ned's porch lamp fell, *à la* Latour, upon my face. Alicia never faltered. Her sheaf of hair beclouded the light; she slammed the door, snuggled and shrugged into place behind the wheel, caused the motor (against its better judgment) to start, and set us afloat through the empty rectilinear streets.

I doubted that she had seen me.

But she sniffed and said, after (from the mix of lights and motion in the back seat) some intersections had been passed and corners turned, "Really, Tom. This won't do."

I sat up. "How was it? How is he? I've been telling Jane he was impotent."

"He *said* you'd been pushing Jane at him. That's pathetic, Tom."

"It was just a thought. How else can you and I go off and run the Boro-boro mission school all by ourselves?"

"We can't and won't."

"Agreed. Taxi, take me home."

I didn't like her tone or the tone it was forcing on me. I began to whine, to rage, to wriggle deeper into the loser's comfortable hole. "You bitch. You flaming harlot. How could you do this to me?"

"Take you home?"

"Screw Bork all the time."

"It hasn't been all the time, Tom. Just a few times. I had to do something to break my obsession with you. I need all the help I can get."

"And does Bork give all the help you can take?"

She sat prim at the wheel. Occasional carlights set her hair on false fire. It had been freshly brushed and neatened, I noticed, which made her recent tussle so real I bent forward to pinch off the pain. I gasped. Only her voice could salve that pain. Each potion its own antidote. She pronounced flatly, "I have no intention of describing it to you. I didn't ask you to spy on me."

"Christ," I grunted, "how could I not, you parked your big black cunt of a car right under my nose! The last time it was there I came down and looked in the window and saw your abso*lute*ly naked foot."

Alicia said, "The last time? I don't think we made love that time, we were just talking. I remember. I took off my shoes and put them up because his floor is so cold. Whosever idea was it, to make a place to live in out of a cement-floor garage?"

"Not mine," I said, undeflected. "Not last time, but this time, is that what you're saying?"

"Is it? You spy, you guess."

"Well. How's the beard? Isn't it awfully tickly?"

"Not too."

This made it real again, her giving her body to another, just when my fantasy of Ned's homo- or asexuality was inching from the realm of faith into a kind of negative verification; I groaned—involuntarily, for I felt, correctly, that I had used up my groans, and the next one would goad her to anger. Without turning, Alicia pulled out the *Tirade* stop and her voice went up on its hard little pipes. "Well how do you think *I* feel, watching you and Jane make cow eyes back and forth every Sunday, what do you think it does to *me,* having you run in and fuck and hop back into your clothes and traipse off to some adoring deaconess after you've had your

11

fun"? "Way with me"? "Kicks for the week"? I forget exactly how she put it. Her complaints went on: my uxoriousness, my pastoral offices, my sense of order and obligation all turned into reproaches, into a young bawd's raillery, and I sat behind her sunk in sadness, sunk deeper each moment as her plaint widened from the justified to the absurd (I even *looked* like my wife; I was planning to seduce Mrs. Harlow; I was going to fire her, Alicia, as soon as she stopped "shelling out"); as she berated me, disclosing all the secret ignominy our affair had visited upon her, and voicing all the shaky hardness that thirty years of being a female in America had produced, a glum ministerial reality overtook my loverly fury and fancies. This woman was a soul in my care. She was crying out, and I must listen—listen not in hope of curing, for our earthly ills elude all earthly ease, but as an act of fraternity amid children descended from, if not one Father, certainly one marriage of molecular accidents. And indeed in some minutes her devils, outpouring, did take up residence in swine, the dark houses flying by, and pass from us. Still controlling the wheel, Alicia sobbed.

I clambed* from the chill back seat to the seat beside her; warmth gushed from the heater onto my legs and face. "I'm sorry," I said, "I'm sorry. It was wrong, our getting each other into this."

"I can't feel that," she said, her syllables prismed by tears.

"Well, something's wrong," I pointed out, "or you wouldn't be crying and I wouldn't be running around in the middle of the night in my pajamas."

She turned her head, at last, and looked at me, very quickly. "Is that true?"

"Just the top," I conceded. "I took the time this time to put on pants. And even a hat. My mother gave it to me."

"Does it upset you that much? My seeing Ned."

"Seems to. Like I say, I'm sorry. Take it as a compliment."

"What do you want me to do?"

"Nothing. Keep at it. Fuck away."

"You know, you've played this awfully cool. You've never once suggested you might leave Jane.

* I must have meant "climb" or "clambered," but which? Kind of a clamby episode in any case.

I know you can't, but even so, it would have been nice, to me, if you'd just once said you *wanted* to."

"She had to give me a reason, and she won't. She's just too good."

"Not in bed, evidently."

"That may not be her fault. Women are cellos, fellows the bows. Anyway, you and I wouldn't be that good either, if it were aboveboard and for day after day instead of an hour a week."

"I love you, Tom. Do you love me?"

"I hate the word, but sure. I'm wild about you, to be exact."

"What do you want from me? Tell me."

"Take me home. To my home," in case she misunderstood. She had been driving into the darkened gumbo of commerce between our two towns, and backed around in the lot of a factory-reject shoestore. No pair alike. If it pinch, wear it. If it feel good, cast it out.

"I'm sorry about Ned," she said after silence. "I hope for his sake I didn't do it just to bug you."

"Is the past tense the right one?"

"I don't know." I feared she would cry again. But we were close to the church and parsonage. There was a dead space of asphalt between them. She stopped here, far from any streetlight, and I wondered if I was meant to kiss her good-night. It seemed strange, to be kissing right to left, the woman behind the wheel. She dropped her hands to my lap and, as intent as when Buxtehude was challenging her fingers with sixteenth notes, unzipped my fly. Miraculous woman! Not a word was spoken; I roused instantly. She unwedged herself from behind the wheel, maneuvered out of her underpants, made of her crotch a Gothic arch above my lap. Imagine: the thickness of our overcoats, the furtiveness of our flesh, the vaporishness of our breaths, the frosted windows through which the turrets and cupolas and dormers of the neighborhood loomed dim and simplified as wicked castles in a children's book. She was wet (a star winked on as I entered her) and ready; I came quickly as I could, she seemed to come, I rezipped, we kissed, I exited, a patch of ice nearly slipped me up, I recovered balance, her headlights wheeled, my house loomed, my weariness wrapped itself around a dazed and dwindling pleasure.

My porch. My door. My stairs. Again the staircase rose before me, shadow-striped, to suggest the great brown back of a slave; this time the presentiment so forcibly suggested to me my own captivity, within a God I mocked, within a life I abhorred, within a cavernous unnameable sense of misplacement and wrongdoing, that I dragged a body heavy as if wrapped in chains step by step upward. Jane stirred as I entered our bedroom. As I undressed, a strand of belated jism dripped lukewarm onto my thigh. I used the bathroom in the dark and slid into bed as grateful as one of the damned might be when the jaws of eternal night close upon his fearful restlessness. Prayer had become impossible for me. "See any UFOs?" Jane, knowing I had been up, misreading my restlessness and taking pity, rolled over, threw a solid thigh across my hip, fumbled for my penis, found it, and would not let go.

My subsequent attitude toward Ned can fairly be described as morbid. That this pale, slight body (which he insisted on garbing, but for unmistakably ceremonial occasions, in affected imitation of youth's glad rags) had the power of copulating with my beloved's—with the body, forgive the Plotinian language, of my soul—fascinated me; his very skin (not, as I have recorded, his best feature) glowed with the triumph. That he took his triumph casually heightened his corrupt glory in my (admittedly; this therapy must be working) diseased eyes. Here was a young man to whom, in indolent footnote to his vows, fornication was a bodily incident no more crucial than spitting. His tactile intrusion into, and escape from, the deep vault of my passion gave him a for me Lazarene fascination—he moved in my vision with the unhealthy phosphorescence of a raised corpse. His body, that is, had blindly entered a charmed circle. I was still his superior, and my knowledge of his secret, where he had none of mine, improved my advantage. But the sum of all this was intimacy. Heaven forbid, I began to love him.

Or at least began to listen. His views, which I had earlier dismissed as hopelessly compromised by topical fads, as the very image of the tower of Babel Barth says our merely human religiosity erects, now had some interest for me.

Ned was engaged with not only our parish youth but also that of the town; he dealt with drug users, above whose abysmal severance from our specifically human gifts of volition and organized effort my spirit hung paralyzed and appalled. "You regard them," Ned told me, with a little surprise, "as untouchables."

"Haven't they," I asked, "declared all of us, the society around them, as untouchable?"

"You've made an image in your mind," he told me. "The drug-oriented kid is more enterprising than his peers, in all the old-fashioned work-ethic ways: he hustles, he sets up contacts, the merchandising system is at least as efficient as Sears Roebuck. A drug addict is a busy, busy fellow. He must learn to burgle, to fence, to con the police, to argue in court. The technology some of these kids can use is remarkable. Just to shoot up is a chemistry lesson. Think of it, Tom, as applied chemistry; the chemistry *is* there, we've been putting it there ever since alchemy."

"Exactly. Alchemy, pacts with the devil, shortcuts from lead to gold. Doesn't a certain stink of evil bother you?"

Ned shrugged. "To them it's the highest good. They say, they don't hurt anybody on a nod, it's coming down when the hurt starts. And then it's all their own. Why should we condemn this, when we give Luther his beer and Buddha his *satori* fix underneath the Bo tree?"

"You don't sound as though you're ministering to them, you sound as if you've joined them."

"Well, wasn't it you who was telling me to join the munitions makers?"

"I think I said businessmen."

"Munitions makers are businessmen are munitions makers. The chain from friendly Henry Cog the local watchmaker to napalm has every link in place. Gene Rostow, the only one of Johnson's old gang with the guts to still talk, said it plain in an interview: We went into Vietnam to keep things open, to keep the world open for trade."

"Better open than closed," I offered. "Better Mammon than Stalin." There was beer in my hand, it was a Saturday afternoon in the little house where Alicia had been laid, Kissinger's Houdini-truce had been effected, we were devietnamized and could attempt dispassion where the flames of rage and counter-rage had danced. Ned's furniture, I might say, was beanbag and paper ball tattily mixed with Good Will. It made me feel young to be here.

He said, "Some of our parishioners tell me in the late Sixties you refused to join peace marches."

I wondered if it had been a parishioner, or Alicia. "Insofar as a peace march proclaims peace to be nicer than war, it is fatuous, surely. The question is, short of the Second Coming, is war always the worst possible alternative? The Bible says not. I say not. You're right, I hated the peace bandwagon worse than I hated the war; it was nearer. It was a moral form of war profiteering."

"How so?"

"It was a power push. All the fat cats and parasites of the system poor Johnson was sweating to save—the college boys, the bored housewives, the professors and ministers and the princelings of computer technology—thought they could push the bad old hard-goods barons and their cowboys out of office. It was the new rich versus the old rich, and the new rich saw what the old rich didn't, e.g., freedom's just another word for nothin' else to do. The new rich saw we could do business with the new thugs of collectivism, 1984 was on its way wherever, and thank God Nixon and his knuckleheads won, though I myself couldn't bear to vote for him."

Ned blinked. I was making him tired. "You mean that, including clergymen among the parasites?"

"A man who's had the call," I said, "will cheerfully be a parasite within any monster that lives. Insofar as you and I eat, we serve Mammon. But there may be, there should be, a little something within us that does not eat, that disdains to eat."

"Disdain," he said, "seems behind a lot of what you say. Your political indifference, for instance."

"I'm not indifferent," I protested, "I'm vigorously pro-Caesar. His face is on the coin, look. Render unto him. Do you know who shares the lowest circle of Hell with Judas? Brutus and Cassius. Even there, Caesar outvotes Jesus two to one. Somewhere Barth says, 'What shall the Christian in society *do* but attend to what *God* does.' What God does in the world is Caesar."

"There are no better or worse Caesars?"

"I tend to trust the Caesar that is, as against the Caesar that might be. The Caesar that is, at least has let us live, which the next might not."

"Do you think," Ned asked, sucking on the pipe that went with his drawling, preppy side, "in Stalin's Russia, say, you would have trusted and served *that* Caesar?"

"Probably." I was grateful to him, for seeing this, and stopping me. My head and tongue were whirling with an angry excitement I didn't understand and didn't like.

"You know, this thing with you and Barth," he went on. "They had us read him in seminary. It was impressive, in that he doesn't crawl, like most of the mod-rens." He didn't have to do that, excuse himself from seriousness with gag pronunciations. I could see that in counselling he would still be self-conscious. Irony is the style of our cowardice. "But after a while I began to figure out why," Ned said. "It's atheism. Barth beheads all the liberal, synthesizing theologians with it, and then at the last minute whips away the 'a' and says, 'Presto! *Theism!*'

It's sleight of hand, Tom. It sets up a diastasis with nothing over against man except this exultant emptiness. This terrible absolute unknowable other. It panders to despair. I came off of it with more respect for Tillich and Bultmann; it's true, they sell everything short, but after they've had the bargain sale there's something left; they say there's a little *something,* don't you see?"

My love for this man took a submissive form. I wanted him to be wise. I wanted him to grow. There were a dozen ledges in his exposition where one could stage an argument (for instance, the Bible is Barth's *something*), but I went feminine and shrugged: "All I know is when I read Tillich and Bultmann I'm drowning. Reading Barth gives me air I can breathe."

"Well that's what the kids say about pot and smack. You and they have more in common than you know. You both believe there's another world more of a high than this one. And you know where they turn, the ones that kick it, often? They turn to Jesus."

"Lord," I said, half to tease him, half to vent the Barth in me, "I find that depressing."

12

Voici une scène. Où je ne suis pas. I must make an image in my mind, as Ned just said. It happened well after Christmas, perhaps on St. Valentine's Day. I heard two accounts and must synthesize. Worse, I must create; I must from my lousy fantasies pick the nits of truth. What is truth? My fantasies are what concern you? How you do make me preen, Ms. Prynne.

The parsonage living-room. Morning sunlight streaming, shade-tainted, dust-enlivened, from windows east and south. Snowcrusts from last week's storm visible through them. Car roofs peep above plow-heaped snow worn glassy in spots by childish boots. Also visible through the window: houses with conical roofs, dormers, protrusions, scallop shingling, jigsawed brackets, ovals of stained glass tucked up under eave-peaks like single eyes under a massive gingerbread eyebrow; and hedges and shrubs, and a mailbox painted in patriotic tricolor, a birdfeeder hopping with feathered mendicants, a covetously onlooking squirrel, streetsigns, streetlamps, etc., etc. Within, our eyes, shifting from the dazzle, blink away a sensation of gloomy solidity amid hothouse warmth. The fuel shortage is a winter away. Glass-fronted bookcases. Dark-veneered furniture. Chairs padded and studded. Everything neat: table-runners centered, back issues of magazines arranged in overlapping rows on a half-folded gate-leg table. Various translucent *objets,* sentimentally given and as sentimentally retained, throw rainbows and loops of light here and there. Dark oaken staircase visible through arched doorway stage left. Knocks offstage. Footsteps.

Enter, chatting, JANE MARSHFIELD, *in austere yet attractive housedress, and* ALICIA CRICK, *bundled in wool, carrying pastel books of music.*

JANE: At least the sun is out.

ALICIA (*tugging off knit cap and fur-trimmed driving-gloves with faintly stagy, excessive, pained exertions*): Is it?

JANE (*hesitantly, aware that this visit is unusual, though not aware yet of its menace*): I don't know exactly where Tom is, I could try—

ALICIA: I just left Tom. At the church.

JANE: Oh.

ALICIA: I came to talk to you. I came, Jane, to ask you to get Tom off my back.

JANE: How—how do you mean?

ALICIA: In about as coarse a sense as you can imagine. I don't know exactly what you and he share, you're a mystery to all of us, but you must have guessed that he and I have—have been together. Have slept together.

JANE (*sitting down, stunned, but in the next heartbeat gathering herself, with an instinctive hauteur perhaps not quite expected by the other, for battle*): No. I had not guessed.

ALICIA: Then I'm sorry to put it to you so bluntly. But I'm desperate. (*She has opted, perhaps because the other's manner has taken some options from her, for a brusque bustly approach, pulling off her scarf, setting down her books, almost stamping her feet, as if to convey a heedless, superior vitality; the effect is rather vulgar, and scatters the plea for sympathy it disguises.*)

JANE (*very gently, after clearing a frog from her throat*): How so?

ALICIA: Your husband is a maddening man. You must know that (*implying, however, that* JANE *doesn't; that she furthermore knows nothing about him* [*me*]).

JANE (*diffidence being her second line of defense*): I don't know, is he really? Around the house, he's been quite cheerful lately.

ALICIA: Now you know why. May I sit down, Jane?

JANE: Please, Alicia, do. Would you like some coffee? Or a little sherry? I know it's still morning, but this seems a rather special occasion.

ALICIA: No, thanks. I can't stay.

JANE: Yet you've taken off your coat. When did this —your—liaison with Tom begin?

ALICIA: After last Easter. Ten months ago.

JANE: And how often did you—usually meet?

ALICIA (*beginning to dislike her responsory role, yet unable to locate where she lost the initiative*): Once a week, more or less. Summer was difficult, with everybody's kids home. When mine were in Minnesota with Fred—my ex-husband—

JANE: I know of Fred.

ALICIA:—Tom and I saw a lot of each other. The rest of the summer, hardly at all. Don't feel sorry for me. There were other consolers.

JANE: Does Tom know this, that there were other men?

ALICIA (*balked almost into angry silence, her anger having to do with* JANE'S *picking up this point so quickly, and with resistance to the agreeable, sliding sensation, not foreseen, of confiding in another woman*): He guesses.

JANE (*considerately seeking to ease her guest's way*): And you wish to end this one of your affairs, the one with Tom?

ALICIA: Why do you say that?

JANE: Why else would you come and tell me? What did you say your object was?—some all too-vivid phrase, to "get him off your back"? (*discovering irony; the whole situation is roomier than she would have believed*) I suppose I can chain him to the bedpost at night, but in the day, he must be out and about—

ALICIA (*she can't have this*): One thing you don't understand. I love Tom.

JANE: And these others—?

ALICIA: And he loves me. We do something very real for each other. Very real and rare.

JANE: You think it my duty, then, to bow out, to vacate (*hands uplifted, with exasperating delicacy, to indicate the walls and furniture about her*) the parsonage?

ALICIA: I think it *his* duty to shit or get off the pot.

Jane vowed to me those were her exact words; I made her repeat them until we both fell to laughing. Their interview, also, fell apart after this exclamation; Jane's distaste, all the more in that she tried to conceal it, flustered my dear organist with her thick waist and firm hands and cogitative cunt. Having trespassed, having blundered, having failed to gain the violent release from ambiguity she had come for, having even forgotten why she had come, she left, cradling her pastel music with the gloves trimmed in fox fur, almost falling on the icy lower porch step, where the eaves always dripped, in her tear-blind rage at her own mistake, at Jane's gracious obstinacy, at our tough marriage. She had seen we were a pair, but had taken us for a salt and a pepper shaker, not the matched jaws of a heartbreaker.

Jane, Alicia gone, poured herself enough of the offered sherry for the two of them, went upstairs, drew a bath, and thrashed hysterically in the steaming, startled water. But she did not attempt to reach me, at some checkpoint of my tortuous rounds, and she met her own afternoon obligations, which were a luncheon meeting of the local garden club, with slides of Elizabethan gardens; a trip to the orthodontist with Martin, my older son; and the reception at four-thirty, of the piano teacher, who audited my younger son Stephen's sullen hammering of some simplified Bartok. I returned at dusk, having during that long afternoon counselled an impending marriage and an impending divorce, having encouraged the Distaff Circle at their quilt-making and driven thirty miles to visit the hospital room of a carcinoma-riddled parishioner who, with his last surge of vitality, bitterly resented my intrusion. To top it all off, this sundae of junk deeds, I had a beer with Ned.

Supper done and the boys safely stupefied by television, Jane said to me, "I suppose your girl friend told you the news."

"What news?" An unfortunate lag. "What girl friend?"

"Alicia dropped by this morning. We had a pleasant chat but she refused sherry. So I've been drinking sherry all day."

"Did she—?"

"Spill the beans? Yes."

What flashed upon me was, I'll never sleep with her again, never see her riding me in the sunlight again. A radiant abyss, like the divine abyss the Apologists posited to counter the Greek myth of Primal Matter. "Why?" was all I could utter.

"I think to help me know you, and to give us the opportunity to separate. Is that what you want?"

"Lord, no." For all the times I had dreamed of freedom from her, my answer came—nay, was flung—from the heart.

"Why not?" Jane reasonably asked. By the candlelight of the dining-room I perceived that she was shaky, that a sherry bottle had materialized beside her dessert dish. "You can move right in. She has everything you need. A house, a way of supporting herself. It would get you out of the ministry, which would be a relief, wouldn't it? You don't believe any more."

"I do! I believe everything!"

"You should listen to your own sermons sometime." Thus spoke, with easy authority, the daughter of Wesley Chillingworth.

"Did Alicia—did Alicia propose my moving in with her?" It was an enchanted thought, residence in that treeless young development, with its view of the cemetery hill, with my cuddly, gum-chewing wife, who would wear filmy dressing gowns carelessly buttoned and breezy and slippers trimmed with pompons; she would be mine for hour after hour. I would get a job. I would learn to fix cars. I would return to her at sundown with lines of grease in my knuckles and palms. With those same hands I would stroke her willing limbs. Between me and such a vision stood a black wall, utterly solid though utterly transparent: onyx sliced miraculously thin.

"We didn't get that far," Jane said. "We thought it was up to you. She said—" And here her quotation, and my incredulity, and our hilarity, and the vision betrayed. We talked to exhaustion that night; I had a meeting at eight, but returned with haste, for not only was I fascinating to her, as I spilled out the details and near-misses on the other side of the looking glass,* but she to me; for she, too, had ventured, if only mentally, from our nest.

"What did it feel like?" I begged, of her encounter with Alicia, already, not three hours gone since I had denied her (no cock crew), ravenous for the sound of my mistress's name, a glimpse of her gestures even through unfriendly eyes, any morsel of the otherworld in which my supine otherform lay transfigured.

* FYI: I swear, Alicia's name is real, not contrived to fit Wonderland. And the last "m" wanted to be a "k." "Near-Mrs." occurs to me as a homonym of Alicia's plight.

"Oh," Jane said, wanderingly, trying to think back and having had too much sherry to think back through—in my mind's eye we are in our glum and ill-lit bedroom, she is groping for her nightie, a dowdy tent of cotton she must have shopped for in a novel by one of the Alcott sisters—"not so bad. It was like being on stage. She came in with her fists up. I minded it less than I thought I would."

"What was the worst moment?"

"When she said she loved you and you loved her."

"What did you say to that?"

"I said I loved you too. And you loved me."

I cannot imagine her saying it, so I have not put it in. Nor do I remember how, in the vast blur of words we generated that night, I responded to her discomfiting declaration. No more dialogue: I see your blue pencil, Ideal Reader, quivering beneath your blue nose. Jane in deportment was drunk, sad, uncomplaining, rather elegantly rational. Having offered me freedom, she did not cinch my captivity, but left it that I would, when I could get my "priorities arranged" (a dry Chillingworth touch, that), come to a decision, to several decisions. Actually, I had no intention of making any decision that others (read: God) might make for me. I did not even resolve, having decided (or having let God enunciate His decision through me) not to marry Alicia, not to sleep with her; this she decided, as her manner—flat, wry, frosty (her interview with Jane had chastened her rather unbecomingly)—plainly declared, in the subsequent days, as we communicated enough, but no more than enough, to allow our professional relationship to continue. If Alicia, then, took on the minimal, masculine posture of a defensive position, combining the stiffness of one who has miscalculated with that of one who has been wronged, Jane in contrast fluffed up, recurring, many a night, to more sherry and to details of my romance, which, the more it became a farfetched tale of adventure and wonder, made me more and more a hero. That Alicia the unmarried, the free, had liked me as lover was the discreetly unvoiced point of fascination. And when, with the passing of the days, my melancholy reassured her of Alicia's withdrawal, Jane, like a wary kitty slowly satisfied that she has the bowl of milk entirely to herself, began to purr. She confessed, what nineteen uxorious years had not made plain, her body's need for mine. Though I felt my body, in her mind, a kind of shadow of Alicia's, its value enhanced by her secret erotic regard for the other woman (women had just begun to call each other "sister"), I complied. In my darkness there was nothing else. Nothing but this sanctioned rutting. Lying beside her then, my consort sated and snoring, I would panic the panic of the sealed, for the last chink had been closed in the perfect prison of my wife's goodness. She had become "good in bed."

13

An unlucky number, but Sunday. Brethren, can it be that another week has gone by, in this fastness, a week of words, mediocre golf (I had the monster on his back, 80 about to break, I swear it, when the lip of a bunker elongated like an elephant's trunk and pulled into its maw a perfectly hit, if underclubbed, 7-iron; I took two to wedge out and three-putted in my craven rage), plenteous drink, and poker games increasingly luminous, as the Demiurge pumices the cards from underneath and renders them transparent to my intuition? Let us repeat together, *Can it be?*

This morning I propose to preach upon the miracles of Christ. Only in the fervor of terror do we dare reach out to touch this most tender flesh of the New Testament. This flesh, bright as a leper's, which modern preaching, as it whores after the sensational, is yet too fastidious to caress. I do not propose to treat of the miracles performed *upon* our Saviour, such as the Bethlehem star, the Voice and Dove that descended on the occasion of His Baptism, the rattling tin sheet and the rheostatted sun backdropping the Crucifixion, or the Miracle of Miracles, that rolled away the rock of His tomb, and as you will remember from last Sunday confronted Mary with the tomb's emptiness, a vacuity smaller than a mustard seed, from which the aeon-spanning branches of this our great church have grown.

For these wonders are the work of God the Father, the Father of all wonders, who parted light from darkness and as easily parted the Red Sea that Moses and his Israelites might pass from Egypt; from the mighty works of this Being, the summit and ground of all being, He who caused the chariot of Apollo to rise from the east for the ancients and who causes the quasars to emit gamma rays for us, we can draw nó lesson, but that—a splendid lesson—He is not ourselves. From the solar miracles of the Father let us turn our scorched vision to the lunar miracles of the Son, miracles that impenetrate a mortal, historical course erratically documented some few generations afterwards.

My consideration must proceed from memory. What a paradox it is, dearly beloved, in a nation where every motel room unavailingly offers a Bible for the perusal of travelworn salesmen, bickering vacationers, and headlong fornicators secluded with eager fornacatrices, that this passel of disgraced and distracted ministers should be uniquely denied the consolation and stimulation of this incredible, most credible book!

For the text of our sermon, let us take the words of Jesus when His mother, anxious that the wedding at Cana go well, importuned Her son, whose unique powers must hitherto have been their guarded domestic secret, to perform His first public miracle. He looked at her astonished and said, "Woman, what have I to do with thee? Mine hour is not yet come."

Mine hour is not yet come. Which well consorts with those of His words recorded in Mark, when, having "sighed deeply in his spirit," He asked the besieging Pharisees, "Why doth this generation seek after a sign? Verily I say unto you, There shall no sign be given unto this generation."

O ye of little faith—this is His cry, for in truth we are insatiable of miracles, and He flees us, as He fled the multitude He had miraculously fed with five barley loaves and two small fishes; yet we of the multitude pursue Him, though He walk on the water to escape us (this according to John), and on the other shore in exasperation He turns, and delivers the accusation, "Ye seek me, not because ye saw the miracles, but because ye did eat of the loaves, and were filled."

And what a fine judgment, by the way, this is of our vaunted American religiosity! From the first Thanksgiving, ours is the piety of the full belly; we pray with our stomachs, while our hands do mischief, and our heads indict the universe.

There once thrived, in that pained and systematic land of Germany, a school of Biblical scholarship that sought to reduce all of the Biblical miracles to natural happenings. The Red Sea's parting was an opportune low tide, and the feeding of the five thousand—the only miracle attested to in each of the four Gospels—was Jesus shaming the multitude into bringing out from under its multitude of cloaks a multitude of box lunches hitherto jealously hoarded. This school of exegetical thought observes that our Lord, before healing the blind man of Bethsaida, spit upon His hands—as if saliva is an attested medication for glaucoma. It notes, with a collusive wink, that the saline density of the Dead Sea is so high that one can virtually "walk" upon it—without noting that Peter, attempting the same maneuver, sank. It whispers the magic word "psychosomatic"—as if Lazarus merely fancied he was dead, the swine spontaneously decided to go for a swim, and the fig tree withered under hypnosis. The absurdities of such naturalism need no belaboring.

Yet a true insight resides in this naturalism. For our Lord produced miracles as naturally as the Earth produces flowers. Miracles fell from Him as drops of water escape between the fingers of a man drinking from his cupped hands. They came in spite of Himself; there is scarcely a one that was not coaxed out of Him—by His mother, by a disciple, by the hunger of a throng, by the unignorable beseeching of an invalid. For Jesus walked in that Roman Palestine upon a sea of suffering. Of the diseases He condescended to cure, there are named blindness, dumbness, dropsy, leprosy, impotence, fever, deformity, issue of blood, madness—a piteous catalogue, and no doubt partial.

It is here, not upon the plausibility of these miracles—they happened as surely as any event in the Gospels happened—but upon their selectivity, that we stumble. If these few, why not *all* the ailing from the beginning of human time? More, of animal time? Why, indeed, institute, with vitality, pain and struggle, disease and parasitism? Reading of the woman with her "issue of blood for twelve years"—twelve years!—who came from behind and touched the hem of His garment, believing, and truly, that this mere touch would make her whole, are we not angry? Angry not at her impudence, but angry that this plucking, this seeking out, this risk of humiliation, was demanded of her, when Omnipotence could have erased her pain as automatically as stony ground lets wither its weeds? Are we not moved to revolt and overthrow this minute and arbitrary aristocracy of the healed, which by chance lived in the three years of our Lord's wandering ministry and by aggression pushed themselves forward into His notice? Do we not cry, with the synagogue at Nazareth, "Whatsoever we have heard done in Capernaum, do also here in thy country"?

And does He not answer, infuriatingly, "Many lepers were in Israel in the time of Eliseus the prophet; and none of them was cleansed, saving Naaman the Syrian"?

And are we not moved, now as then, to rise up, and thrust Him out of the city, and lead Him to the brow of the hill, that we might cast Him down headlong, so that He might taste, with us—us the drowning man, the starving man, the falling man—might taste the implacability of natural laws that do not suspend an atom of their workings however huge and absolute the cry of our appalled spirits?

And, now as then, He passes through our midst invisible, ungraspable, and goes His way.

For His way is not ours.

The hard lesson is borne in upon us, alleviation is not the purpose of His miracles, but demonstration. Their randomness is not their defect, but their essence, as injustice (from our point of view, which is that of children) is essential to a Creation of differentiated particulars. In the primal partition of darkness from light, the potential for better and worse was born, and with it the possibility of envy and pain, process and loss, sin and time. He came not to revoke the Law and Ground of our condition but to demonstrate a Law and Ground beyond.

Let us examine His miracles further. Not all of them heal. Along with the miracles of mercy, which as we see are wrung from Him, not from the strength of His Divinity but from the weakness of

His humanity, there are the festive miracles, and, more edifying still, the facetious miracles.

Festivity merges with mercy in the feeding of the thousands, who would otherwise have experienced discomfort. In the turning of the water into wine at the wedding at Cana, and in the miraculous draught of fishes that breaks the net and nearly sinks the boat, festivity acquires a comic note, and prepares us for the comedy of His walking upon the water while Peter sinks, an Abbott and Costello routine at a far stylistic remove from the W. C. Fieldsish blasting of the fig tree and the Chaplin-esque ballet of the graceful episode wherein Jesus, queried by his tireless straight man Peter about local taxes, sends the fisher of men to catch a fish and finds in that fish's mouth a coin which is then handed—we can almost see the winsome pursed lips of the cosmic Tramp—to the tax collector!

Let us become Jesus for these moments. Let us seek empathy with the Son of God who, as He was truly man, and who underwent the crucifixion in uncertainty and dread, must have conceived this mad prank, of looking for money in the mouth of a random fish, with some dubiousness; yet it worked. Or imagine yourself Him when, in His first miracle, His powers green and unproven, He bid the servants fill the waterpots with water to the brim and bear them unto the governor of the feast. Suppose the water had not become wine but still proved, in the governor's mouth, water? This would be comedy too, but of another kind; a grim and pratfallen kind —our mortal kind.

When we thus empathize, at what do we marvel? His daring. His faith. "O thou of little faith," He cries to Peter as Peter sinks beneath the waves, and when the disciples, the Evangelist Matthew tells us a few chapters later, could not cure the lunatic who "falleth into the fire, and oft into the water," Jesus thunders at them, "O faithless and perverse generation, how long shall I be with you?" and tells them, His anger cooled, that "If ye have faith as a grain of mustard seed, ye shall remove mountains; nothing shall be impossible unto you."

Well, are we not such a faithless and perverse generation? A generation of falling men, of starving men, of bleeding women, of drowning Peters? Imagine a man married to goodness, and hating the goodness as darkness hates the light; yet he cannot budge that marriage and his hate by a thumb's-width, and his spirit curses God. Why has the perfect and playful faith that Christ demonstrated in His miracles never come again, though saints have prayed in these two thousand years, and torturers have smiled?

Dearly beloved, let us open ourselves to this lesson. I feel you gathered beneath me, my docile suburban flock, sitting hushed in this sturdy edifice dedicated in the year 1883 and renovated under my canny predecessor in the year 1966. Strong its walls were built; with metal rods and extruded concrete were they reinforced. But let us pray together that its recollected and adamantine walls explode, releasing us to the soft desert air of this Sunday morning a thousand and more miles away. Nay, not explode, but atomize, and vanish noiselessly; nay, not that either, but may its walls and beams and mortar turn to petals, petals of peony and magnolia, carnation and chrysanthemum, and as at one of the infamous feasts of Baal-adoring Heliogabalus collapse in upon us, melting walls of perfume and color and allurement, so that each female among you is graced with a sudden orgasm and each man of you receives at least a hint, a mitigating hint, that the world is not entirely iron and stone and effort and fear. Let us pray for that. Let us confidently expect that. For there must be, in this sea of pinched and scrubbed Sunday faces, a single mustard seed of faith.

There is not. The walls stand. We are damned. I curse you, then, as our Lord cursed the fig tree; may you depart from this place forever sterile; may your generation wither at the roots, and a better be fed by its rot.

Amen.

14

Mrs. Harlow's fragile, appealing face across my desk from me. Me trying to keep my thoughts up from her bosom, which her knit dress is hugging snugly enough to warm a saint. Her voice floats out and upwards from her face's delicate net, escaping to be drowned in the air from the open window, open to a bonny slushy day, of false spring, the trappings of winter melting, March. Another Lent. ". . . and he really loves me so much, it's quite touching, I feel such a, such a *vill*ainess."

From her pause, I am to say something. As little as possible at this stage. I am counselling. "I think we should get our feelings out, before we begin censoring them."

This braces her, brings her an inch more upright and nearer to me. She girds to say the unspeakable. "I *loathe* his touch," she tells me. "I'll think of any excuse, a headache, stomach trouble, I feign sleep"

—her vocabulary has about it a touch of the old-fashioned valentine; her diction is as distinct as her shape—"and he always understands, and forgives, it's quite ex*ac*erbating. I'd rather he'd beat me, leave me, be a *man*—"

My impulse is to reach across the desk and slap her face. She must sense this, for she halts, her smooth gray eyes alarmed. "Go on," I say. Into my abrupt boredom the sound of cars swishing on the melting street pours as if a volume switch had been turned.

She slumps, surrenders the inch closer she had come. "I can hardly elaborate further. I don't *really* want him to beat me, I'd despise him if he did; but it would be an *act*ion, you see, it would be a—shattering."

"Oh?"

"I beg your pardon?"

"What is it, Mrs. Harlow, that you feel would be shattered?"

With her fine dry skin in her soft knit dress, she senses an abrasive resistance where I, as minister, should be all divine compliance, a vacuum where she can expand. It excites her, my resistance. Her sensing it excites me. Her answer, when she comes up with it, is good. It has a coin in its mouth. She proclaims, wider-eyed, "Why, our grotesque false peace! I cannot *stand* this man, and nobody knows it. Except you."

"I'm not sure I do know that." I shift in my chair.

"When did these feelings of distaste begin? Obviously they weren't there when you married."

"Why would that be obvious?" I like her fondness for the subjunctive. We are circumscribed by tangents. She knows that.

"Why would you have married Mr. Harlow otherwise?"

"Because everybody I knew was getting married and I didn't want to be alone!"

"And *are* you alone?"

"I'm more alone *with* him than I would be with*out* him."

"He loves you."

"He doesn't *know* me. How can you love what you don't know? His love is insulting. It's stupid. Reverend Marshfield, I cannot believe love has to be so stupid."

"You can afford to feel insulted," I tell her, "because he protects you." Children returning from school shout in the acoustic wet street. "You and your children," I remind her.

Mrs. Harlow—her first name is Frances, we call her Frankie—comes so swiftly forward in her chair I fear she might hiss. "How can you give me," she asks, her voice brittle and true as rods of glass, "this middle-class moralism? I could get this from my husband."

"Well I don't want to give you what your husband would give you," I say.

"I'm a person," she says. "A soul. Why should I

live so dishonestly? Why should I die on my feet just because I've had children?"

"Except a seed dieth," I begin.

"Well I think it's rotten. Tom. I mean that. I think the way I feel I'm just the waste of a human being. And I can't believe the Christian church was instituted to preside over the waste of human beings."

"I can't believe it either," I say, hurriedly, for she has stood up. The snugness of the knit wool about her hips dries my mouth; the sensation is as of an unanatomical emptiness in my chest sucking moisture from my normal cavities, and the emptiness is part (confirmingly, somehow) of a cosmic imbalance.

Her flurry of words races on without me, "And now I have to go home because the damn children are coming home from school, and then the cats need to be fed, and then Gerry comes home from work. Children, cats, Gerry, the dishes, bed. Do you think I should have an affair?"

"Mightn't a part-time job be more constructive?"

"I don't have time for a job! My life is too constructive already!" Her heat embarrasses her; she turns (snug behind as well, in nice balance, liberate Libra) and fluffs herself into her coat, a knee-length mink from more middle-class days. She shoves her smarting pink hands into the pockets and pouts, helpless. I stand, helpless also. My collar bites under the Adam's apple. "Shall I come again?" Her voice lower.

I measure my words. Less a question than a defiance.

"If it helps. You've raised several issues that should be talked through with someone."

"This a good time for you?"

I consult my calendar, suggest that she and her husband might come in together some evening.

"No, goodness," Mrs. Harlow lets out, with a giggle even older than the mink. "He'd kill me if he knew."

She gone, I blink. This interview, like the following, and the preceding (she came to my office, uxoriously troubled, around the time that Alicia staged her scene with Jane), in its shifting transparencies and reflecting opacities, seems an experience so gnostic I am blinded.

O, Ms. Prynne, she was fair and fine and spoiled and open-eyed, the web of time sat like the most delicate purdah upon her face, whereas you are dark and heavyset and militantly competent and uncivil in the hall, which vibrates with your patrolling step: forgive me for tormenting you with fond memories. If I knew what you wanted. If you would leave me a multiple-choice questionnaire as does the Ramada Inn. If you would grant me a sign, disturb the placement of these pages on the dresser top, invert the paper clip I cunningly sandwiched in a northeasterly direction between pages 89 and 90, anything . . . The silence of this room *m'effraie*. It is not one silence but many; the lampshade is silent, the bulb silently burns, the bed in silence waits for my next oblivion, the bathroom mirror silently plays catch with a corner of my bathrobe, the carpeting is a hungry populace of individual acrylic silences, even the air-conditioner, today, is silent. Has the power failed? Has the desert cooled? Has the beautiful last beseeching of the Bible ("Even so, come, Lord Jesus."—Rev. 22.20) been at last answered, and Man's two millennia of Inbetweentimes ended? No, my clock says an hour to noon remains.

How could I leave Jane? How could I make up my betrayal, the lover's perennial betrayal, to Alicia? No way. Any change in circumstances would only have substituted another pang for the pang I felt when, during service, Alicia, looking, in her white surplice over red cassock, remarkably like the sub-teen lads of her choir, but that her hair was a curl longer, bent nearsightedly close above the keyboards of her gorgan* and the beams above us all began to tremble with the whole-note fifths of the *Venite,* or the tripping quarters of the plainsong *Sanctus,* or the preliminary run-through of one of the out-of-the-ordinary hymns she favored, such as

* Thus. My glimpse might turn me to stone?

"O Master of the Callous Hand" or "Behold a Sower! From Afar" or "Come, Ye Disconsolate, Where'er Ye Languish." I would remember then how in another setting she would bend over me, her hands as tepid and untimid as those of a masseuse, and bring me up to pitch, and the throbbing church would swim in the one sea of love that encircles us, that upholds the mailbox on the corner and the Dow-Jones in New York and the starlings on their swiftly portable columns of grace.

I vowed to abjure the word "love," yet write of little else. Let us think of it as the spiritual twin of gravity—no crude force, "exerted" by the planets in their orbits, but somehow simply, Einsteinly there, a mathematical property of space itself. Some people and places just make us feel heavier than others, is all.

In the gaunt and ornate house that Jane and I inhabited until such time as a fresh call would take us away, weightlessness prevailed. Her initial excitation by my adultery and her starring part as Wronged Wife in the post-Christmas pageant had passed; I could feel, now, as the warmer days led me to toss aside the blankets and invite her to attempt a physical attitude airier than the strict vis-à-vis, the moment when remembrance turned her off, when a sensation of being forced into another's mold balked her flow and turned our milk-white bodies sour. I minded less than you may think. An anti-sexual wife whom I had the pleasure of arousing guilt in and a mistress whom I had the pleasure of adoring without the inconvenience of managing trysts and shaking off her clinging afterplay comprised not the worst arrangement in this imperfect world. That both women gave me pain seemed a tidy stroke of spiritual economy. Better, St. Paul said, to marry than to burn; better still to marry *and* burn.

Also Mrs. Harlow seemed to be coming along.

Also my father, who in space-time occupied a stark room of a rest home an hour distant, which he furnished with a vigorous and Protean suite of senility's phantoms, was in a genetic dimension unfolding within me, as time advanced, and occupying my body like, as Colette has written to illustrate another phenomenon, a hand being forced into a tight glove. I was reading less Barth and more Tillich, and had taken to puttering pleasurably about the house.

First try, I typed "putting," which shows where my heart lies. Sorry this is such a lumpy issue. Blue Monday. Yesterday's sermon, so close to putrefying into blasphemy, sits ill on my stomach. Perhaps the *consensus gentium* is correct, there should be things called "mysteries," locked up in Latin and forgotten.

15

Short, bright paragraphs today. Yesterday I successfully eliminated, in all but the clutchiest of shots, my excess of backswing. For an at-moments sparkling 82. Amazing, how powerful a short swing (with some hips into it) can be.

Puttering. For instance, a number of broken sash cords hung from the windows, making them sticky to open and yet liable to fall like guillotines upon the numb skull of one attempting to replace storm panes with screens.* I had never taken apart a window before. What an interlocked, multi-deviced yet logical artifact one is! And how exciting, all the screws unscrewed and stop strips removed, to pull forth from decades of darkness the rusted sash-weight, such a solid little prisoner, and fit him with

* Pains with screams?

a glossy new noose and feel him, safe once again in his vertical closet, tug like life upon the effortlessly ascendant sash! It is positively sexual, this answering quickening from within the carpentered arcanum of the frame.

Or Jane, whose virtue sought symmetry and enclosure, had been long bothered by the absence of a door leading from the foyer into the living-room. There had once been a door there, hinge-butts testified. But the door itself had vanished. But there were other doors, left over from some renovation of the morcenary Morse, in the cellar, displaced to there from the garage when it was in turn renovated. I found one of them sound and, with some planing, to fit. Finding matching hardware, however, was an ingenious work of salvage, that sent me even into the attic, where a solitary brass strike, of obsolete design, waited loose on a sill to be rendered useful to Man again. Other bits—the other half of the hinges, the latch bar—were painted and riddled with rust, and the idle little work, at my cozy bench beside the furnace, of integrating these components, of cleaning them in coffee cans of seething chemicals and fitting them to the patched and puttied door, which had been hinged oppositely from how I intended to hang it, gave me a pleasure perhaps disproportionate to the benefit achieved. It is true, when at last in place, the residual imperfections of my handiwork struck me more forcibly than its skill, and I had a demonic impulse to splinter the whole thing with the hammer warm in my hand from tapping home the hinge pins. But I desisted, habituation soon assuaged me, and Jane was pleased. That I continued to wish, and continue to wish, to please my wife, I append as a sorry frill upon, as an ulcerated blemish beneath the belt of, these confessions. Perhaps Jane's coo of admiration, wrung by my work from her sainted silence, did for my mother's singing.

It occurs to me, remembering the fabled time when I lived in the world and had my being there, that I was infatuated with completion, with the repair in place, the sermon delivered, the ejaculation achieved, the letter mailed; with the deed done rather than, as a healthy hedonism might fatuously advise, with the doing. As a chid* I would put myself to sleep by imagining objects—pencils, hassocks, teddy bears—sliding over a waterfall. I loved shedding each grade as I ascended through school. Even the purgative sweep of windshield wipers gratifies me. A lifelong drive to disrobe myself of circumstances has brought me stripped to this motel. Remember my compulsive hymn to the toilet bowl? Shall we work on that later? Or flush it?

* Sic. Yet as a child I was more ignored than chidden. Perhaps wanted more Jahwehian thunder from Dad? More scolding arias from Mom? Or perhaps Freud's stumblebum God does not impart His dark fingerprint to every slip of the tips.

With Alicia Jane was aloofly correct and, on the occasions when her black Chevrolet, embossed with moonbeams, parked at Ned's house and I suffered, angry on my behalf. "Of *course* she wants you to see, of *course* she wants to hurt you with it," Jane insisted in my ear, when I was lazily inclined to give Alicia the benefit of the doubt and blame my discomfort on a private demon and this visible conjunction on blind chance. After all, I reasoned, she had other lovers, whose houses I did not overlook, so the τελος of her copulation was not to irritate me. Yet when, to rid myself of torment—her appearances at Ned's having become a virtually unbroken *continuo* under the treble of my fitful dreams—I moved to dismiss my unconscionably musical organist, it was Jane who protested, and Ned who blandly agreed and reinforced my will. But to prolong this paragraph might compromise its shortness and brightness.

My ghostly reader telepathically reminds me that I have written unnaturally little of the two other occupants of the parsonage; my offspring, my blood and seed, my Jacob and Esau, my two sons. To call them "vermin" would convey their sleeplessly greedy activity and the gnawing, gutting effect their quarrels, misadventures, and demands worked upon my brain; but it would confer an undue dynamism upon their position in my plight. As I writhed to escape my life, they were agonizing but inert; they were the two galvanized nails in my palms, the unravelling fringes of my threadbare days, the rumpus upon awaking and the headache at bedtime, the unappeasable termites tunnelling to a powdery dust the beams and joists of my time on earth. For are not children exactly that which does not have an ending, which outlasts us, which watches *us* slide over the waterfall, with relief? Society in its conventional wisdom sets a term to childhood; of parenthood there is no riddance. Though the child be a sleek Senator of seventy, and the parent a twisted husk mounted in a wheelchair, the wreck must still grapple with the ponderous sceptre of parenthood.

Martin is sixteen, Stephen fourteen. I have written earlier (find it yourself, you prying Prynne) of a certain tendony sameness Jane and I share; Martin inherited this twofold. Even as an infant in arms he was wiry and would push off from his mother's breast or wriggle from my restraining embrace with the puissance of a wildcat. He excels at all sports, though small, and will amuse us with sudden tricks he has secretly rehearsed, such as kicking a soccer ball with the heel of his foot so it bounces up to his head, or leaping over a broomstick held in his hands, or adroitly catching in midair a button or stack of pennies balanced upon his elbow. Subject to nervous headaches and frighteningly intense stretches of sleep, he is, awake, a jabber, a perfectionist pained to fury by the imperfections around him. No blot sits larger on his horizon than his brother, who is his size, and has been almost from birth. As a fetus Stephen was so ample (ten pounds minus an ounce postpaid) that he frightened Jane away from her plan (which I, with the naïveté of the Fifties, when the global plum pudding, full of dimes and brandy, seemed served up all for Uncle Sam, because he had been so good, shared) of having four children. Our softness, the doughiness of the soul that keeps* us sticking together and mires our essential indignation in the pasty peace of a quiet meal or an evening spent with Bach and a book, has been concentrated in this dear plump child, who would have constructed, for himself, a paradise of model airplanes and collected minerals and introverted musings had not Providence supplied his brother to give evil a physical presence. In toddlerhood, Martin beat upon the offensively large infant as upon an unresonant drum; as they aged, the older boy outraced and tripped up the younger at every game they played; older still, Martin taunted his brother with a barrage of complaints for which, since they seemed to be forced from him by a demon beyond, I could not hold him culpable. Nor could I but pity my tender son even though, as he grew, he developed from his superior bookishness a hectoring legalism in his own defense. I felt all sides; and could help none. My stomach grinds as, moral gears clashing, I hear them debate at table.

* The Marshfields mallow?

"You're disgusting," Martin abruptly announces to his sibling as he sits opposite in the candleglow of dinner.

"Why? What did I do?" Fear slightly overaccents each syllable; fear, and a determination not to be erased from account.

"Mom!" Martin cries, and in the fine pull of his skin at his temples I feel a headache starting. "First he chews with his mouth open, then he talks so you can see all the mush!"

"No worse than you," Stephen counterclaims. "Coming to the table with hands all roguey from playing basketball in the mud and face all pimply so it looks like a pizza."

"Looks like a pizza, ha, ha, smoothie. For your information I cannot help the skin blemishes induced by adolescent glandular changes but you could learn how to chew properly instead of slobbering like a baby."

"For *your* information my nose is all stuffed up so if I close my mouth I can't breathe. At least I don't ruin everybody else's dinner by talking about it and saying Disgusting and all the stuff we've heard before and is boring anyway."

"My, my," Martin says, in truth a little overwhelmed, sidling his eyes toward me to see if it shows. "Listen to the young fellow expostulate."

"At least," Stephen pursues, "I don't keep disgusting copies of *Penthouse* under my bed and have a face all scabs."

Jane asks, "*Can't* the two of you let each other alone for one meal? I'm ashamed of you both. Tom, say something."

I say, "Where does the kid get *Penthouse?*"

Martin, though the meanness of the vexed will always be his, does not have much aptitude for sin; he has my delight in fittingness, but applied to his own body, and now that he has a driver's license he shames me by always fastening the safety belt, and never exceeding the speed limit.

Stephen, on the other hand, so long bullied into a passive goodness, and for too many years of his life angelic-looking, with his baby complexion and long-lashed eyes, has a backlog of temptations he is anxious to adjust. His inwardness will welcome drugs; his beauty will attract girls; and his years of absorbing abuse will excuse him, I fear, from guilt. This meek one is prepared to inherit the earth. He goes to a private school we can ill afford, and shows no shying away from the life of the rich. I picked him up one midnight after a dance and asked him, in the faintly pregnant silence of the car—he seemed perfumed, and affably dazed—how it was. "O.K.," he said. I asked him to elaborate. He snapped, "Groovy. Hassle-free." My, how this saddened me! Welcome, Buddha. Howdy, Nirvana. Adam did not fall, nor did Christ rise, that the world might be hassle-free.

Martin, by contrast, insisted on going to the local public school, without admitting it was for my sake

—to save me money, to make me look community-minded. He is on a team each season and causes our spondaic name to ring from the bleachers. On the anvil of his brother's head he forged himself a backbone. He has aspirations, and expectations; even before my scandal, I embarrassed him, with my overly agonistic sermons, my devious irony, my sense of the priest as fool and scapegoat. He laughs only in triumph—at a goal, a stunt. When the meal is over, he sits at the table tossing crumbs and pellets of paper into empty glasses, and applauds the occasional miracle of ricochet. But it frightens me, the halo of unhappiness around his head. My attempts to talk to him buckle on this fright. My words cease. I remember his kicking out of my arms as a baby. I am timid of touching him, he is too tightly wound, he might break.

Stephen, I might add, with his pliable good looks, was endlessly cuddled, and accepted it, and now stays awake listening to the radio murmur its nothings in darkness; while his older brother, sweating and slack as an unfurled fist, has been dutifully asleep for hours.

My two sons. A more fruitful topic than I had supposed. I had meant to go on to my father today, but noon and the desert, liquor and golf, call. Heredity, it occurs to me, works up as well as down. The creatine of golfing passion did not begin shooting in my muscles until I had an athlete for a son.

Nor did I become a lover until my second son proved beautiful. A jabber and a taker, a Spartan and a Sybarite: the trunk stands declared in its forking.

16

Once a week in theory, less often in practice, I would climb into my clerical brown Dart (if there are Earthgazers in the UFOs, they must see us as a species of mollusc, or perhaps believe that automobiles are our hosts, and we are parasites viable for brief periods of scuttling) and steer a drear hour through America's highway nightmare to the nursing home where my father, seventy-seven years young, was stashed. A rural byway, a crescent of low brick buildings, a euphemistic shingle in gilded woodcraft, *Valleyhead*. Within, an all-denying cleanliness. A stout receptionist, magenta cashmere sweater worn capelike atop nurse's starched bodice, smiles at the kindred arc of my collar; how girls go for a uniform! Down rubber halls hung with *trompe-l'œil,* doorway-sized examples of neo-realism depicting shrivelled staring oldsters waiting for No One between sheets of white. The verisimilitude is breathtaking. The innocent rows of a nursery, of a poultry broodery; each room held a live soul hatching the egg of its rounding, and beckoned me vaporously in, and would have ensnared me in pity and love had I not strode stern, eyes locked against trompery, toward the far cell where sat a magical man who once claimed to be my father.

But no more. His claims had ceased. He confused me with his brother Erasmus, with an old Army mate called Mooney (my father had served in the First World War, not as chaplain but as fighting private, whose battalion disembarked in France in the first week of November 1918, and stayed for six months of riotous peace in the raped villages of Picardy), with several interchangeable m.c.'s who ran daytime television quizzes and exhibitions of middle-class pawkiness, with the obscure power behind and above this slippery establishment in which he found himself, and, obscurer and more ominous still, with some man who, he seemed to believe, threatened to steal my mother from him. My father tended to move through these confusions in the order of my listing; so our interviews went from fraternal cordiality to frightened antagonism. The fright mine, not his: my tolerance for unreality, supernaturalist though I claim to be, turns out to be low. That he looked at me and saw someone else turned my bones to water. Hung with thoughts no more rooted than mistletoe, his head was still massive and unlike mine (my mother's skimpy genes) still woolly: not only had he lost scarcely a strand to time but his hair, rarely cut by the authorities, had grown richer in wildness, curlier, as dense and candid as a ram's fleece. His mouth, his nose, his nostril-hairs—everything had grown but his eyes, which a swelling in the surrounding flesh had reduced to a beady, ingeniously frantic, rather Mongolian slant. He would be sitting beside his steel bed in an armchair with wooden arms, wearing a plaid bathrobe Jane and I had given him. Jarringly, the cloth of the armchair was virtually the same plaid; it gave his presence an electric penumbra of displacement, like the vibrant aura surrounding film actors superimposed upon a background that is in fact another film running.

"Thank the Lord, you've arrived at last!" His great voice, with its mellow country vowels and crisp way of darkening and deepening at the end of a phrase, had survived into senility to give even his most nonsensical utterance the hollow sonorousness of sermons I had squirmed through thirty years before. "In the fullness of time," he went on, in a mode more sarcastic, "the bridegroom cometh. We've been waiting by this fool barn an eternity, I thought the shade would turn to vinegar." He heard the tone of a witticism in these words, and his little eyes hardened in expectation of my laughter.

I obliged. "I come whenever I can," I added.

"Then don't make appointments you can't keep," he promptly responded. "Brother's keeper, bet your bottom dollar. If our father saw you stealing apples, you'd have a hiding to make your britches glow. Did you bring me any booty?"

"How would this do?" A box of Schrafft chocolates, bought at a drugstore in a shopping center on the way. His spotted square hands tore at the cellophane like a raccoon's paws; his appetite for food, far from diminishing, as it would in some ordered phasing-out, had grown with the decay of his mind, and aided the illusion that his body was swelling in strength and presence. The backs of his hands were spattered with large moles, ancestors of the moles that had begun to emerge on the backs of mine.

He put a chocolate cherry into his mouth, and followed it too soon with a chewy caramel; excess stained his lips darkly. *You're disgusting,* I thought of telling him. With messy mouth he roguishly told me, "You have a sweet tooth, Ras. Not to mention" —two sugar-coated almonds flew after the caramel, and were crunched—"a sweet lookout for *les filles des villes*"—pronouncing each word disyllabically, with a rhyming *ee-yah*—"*n'est-ce pas?* Tell me true, how was that little filly with the big knockers? Big above, slow below, that's the rule of thumb. Give me a bitty narrow-assed slip of a thing every time, make every man feel a beast, good things in small packages, can you fault me there?"

The baseness of his undressed mind shocked me. My mother had been a small woman.

"Don't sit there slack-jawed as a moron, Mooney, confess your sins with a ready heart. After what we've been through the Lord holds us entitled to a little *plaisir,* a little animal easement. Body and soul, soul and body, the lion and the lamb shall lie down together, and there is no afterlife. Any preacher's son can assure himself of that, just read your molecules. Tell me about the little black-haired twat, might try her myself. *Mam'selle, mam'selle, beaucoup de dollair si vous allez au lit avec moi,* it gets them where they live, losers can't be choosers. What is it these frogs say, *le con est le centre du monde.* You know what my tart told me they call an engagement—a *compromis.* Hear it? *Com-promis!* A promised cunt! And these were innocent village girls four short years ago. Mooney, you're not laughing. You're homesick."

I told my father, "I'm thinking over the wisdom of your words."

"And well you might, you laggard. Homesick, prick-sick, Mooney, you're sickly, and that's no mistake. Deceit has done you in. That's the trick about sin, it does in the doer. You think you've got on top of me, the hard fact is I've got on top of you. I'm accumulating evidence, and not a court of decency in the commonwealth can fail to uphold me. The vestry concur in this course of action. Even though it may cost a pretty penny, we've agreed to touch the Discretionary Fund." A flicker of suspicion that his scheme—his sensation that a scheme was in motion—might be slipping awry, might indeed have a false bottom the size of perdition, faded from his face at the thought of the Discretionary Fund. He had attained firm ground. He resettled in the chair; the edges where the two nearly matching plaids met vibrated. He crossed his legs, and a long mauve shin showed, rubbed hairless to the height of a man's socks. Betraying the tousled vigor of his head, his ankles looked bloodless. They were a cadaver's denerved stems. My father said, his hands pressed into his lap to suppress their trembling, "The truth of it is, they need me out there. Otherwise, I'd let you have your freezer, and go for the Exxon jackpot with my eyes tight shut against all these ramifications."

"Daddy, who needs you out there? Who do you mean?"

He looked at me fishily, and groped on the bed for his pipe. They had taken it away from him, for burning holes in his blanket. He did not like my calling him "Daddy," nor did I. But he had no other name; "Father" had been our name for God. Squinting obliquely, having turned his head to help grope for the non-existent pipe, he asked me, "Must we always have that vacuous little smile? Is there no surcease from this artificial good humor, this charade of good will?"

"I'm sorry," I said, meaning it, feeling fear grow in me while a prickly righteousness, a kind of invisible hair, began to rise on him.

"Who? You ask me who?" He thought the answer would be obvious, but found it not so; his stare of scorn narrowed to canniness. "Why, all of them. Out there. In Viewerland." He gestured toward the television set, silent and gray-faced behind me. "The meetings," he expatiated, "their many petty concerns as they move from birth to death, and meet their tragedies and difficulties, the disappointments of freedom, the profound fulfillments of the middle way, the ills that flesh is heir to. Its warp and weft comprises the fabric of a parish, and I am the shuttlecock," he told me, and, pleased with the echo of happiness in this phrase, leaned toward me with heavy confidentiality. "It is not that you do my poor person wrong by this obstructionism; it is that you deprive the many others of what weak wisdom the Gospel of Love might shed."

I was tempted, I fell in with his phantoms. "We all agree, though," I said, "that *this* is the place for your ministry. You have done wonderful work here. Of course, if you *want* to move on, but do you feel that your work is completed?" I gestured at the blank walls, the tightly made bed with its side-rails, the dead television set. The room smelled of ammonia. "Can't you feel it, how you are surrounded by need, and by admiration?"

His head at first had nodded agreement, but by the end of my speech, as my voice flattened against these bare walls, he knew something was amiss. He looked at me with a look a son should never see upon his father's face, the face the father turns away from the home and presents to the enemies outside. "You call it admiration," he growled, "I call it covetousness, and adultery. You and she have wounded me beyond the power of words to express, but I will not be trodden upon. I am no poor worm. I have no such intention, sir. I am disabused, sir. *Damn* your business connections. *Damn* your friends in high places."

I fought down the fear fluttering behind my face; I half-rose, expecting a blow.

With ponderous steadiness, he went on, "I have never liked you, to be frank. You have a cowardly and lecherous smell. I held my nose the moment you came into my house. Though you have powerful allies, I am not powerless. There are legal steps. There is other recourse. Though I never killed, I was once a soldier, and would have killed. I love life too much to be a pacifist. She knows the depth of my feeling. She knows how you used her. You will say she used you in turn. I have heard men say such filthy things. This is how you repay her, with filth."

"Daddy," I said, "I don't know what you're talking about. I'm your son. Mother is dead. She loved only you."

His handsome, heavy face congested; his eyes, smaller than a pig's and cloudy as phlegm, looked through me yet at me with a fury of intent. "Do you want me," he said, and every word trembled with its overburden of passion, "to hurl this sacred book"—

the box of chocolates—"right into your face?" I fled.

From outside the room, in the hall, I looked back and saw him, his handsome face mottled, stare at the space where I had been and with an air of absentminded satisfaction take a nougat from the box and pop it, still wrapped in waxpaper, into his mouth.

In the same time of my life as this interview, Mrs. Harlow led me, her hand trembling and the palm damp, down into her den. The Harlows lived on the outskirts of town, where the two-acre building lots were wooded and expensive, in a newly built ranchhouse so modernistically glassy there felt to be no corner in its rooms where one might embrace unseen. We had just kissed behind the door, as I tried to leave, my mouth tasting of the coffee with which, irreproachably, she had rewarded my irreproachable call, having to do with the Whitsunday flower display of the Distaff Circle or some such trompery. Her own mouth had been a startling many-petalled bloom of more lips than two and more tongues than one. I melted and froze; the den was down carpeted stairs and floored with maroon rubber and walled with knotty pine and littered with mock-leather furniture and outsize children's toys, billiard tables wide as a lawn and dart boards the height of a man. Giants rumpussed here. She renewed the kiss, producing upward from her throat and the well of her deep being more excited petals of tongue and touch; I felt passive as a sleeper; edges of cloth, silk parting from skin, grazed my fingers; she stood before me naked. She was taller than Alicia and frailer than Jane; the veil of wrinkles upon her face extended no further; her body was as smooth as her gaze. Only something peakèd, an anxious shapely skinniness in the glossy jut of ilium and clavicle, hinted she was more than girl. I let her undress me as one would a dummy (the stud at the back of my collar a problem as always) and felt exalted holding her nakedness in the arms of mine. But no erection arose. The experience was so new to me I scarcely had the grace to be abashed. Perhaps her jutting, fluttering eagerness left me no space to grow in; her husband's exercise bicycle beside the rack of pool cues didn't help. Harlow was a cherished deacon from my predecessor's go-go days, a stocky gray-jawed bank executive with a formidable way of withholding his smile one judicious second and then showing even his gold molars in a braying I've-got-you laugh. I was too aware of my car parked visibly outside and Mrs. Harlow felt fragile to me, a fevered child in my care. Unlike Jane and Alicia, she was a believer. She held my limp penis in her hand and called me lovely. Her forgiveness and the pre-Adamic, cave-woman fall of her hair to her bared shoulders broke a capsule inside me. I felt my heart spill, while my penis hung mute. In the house above us, a machine switched itself on. Had it been God's footstep, there was no escaping from this nether zone. I dropped to my knees, a pro at that, and arranged her hands tangent as in prayer in front of her pudenda—a startling dark curly copper, quite unrelated to the hair of her head—and kissed her hands' dry backs and turned them over and kissed their moist palms, their moisture and my immanence of tears mingling; spouting comical vows to come again in glory, I dressed and left. At the foot of the cellar stairs I paused and saw her posed, my lovely Frankie Harlow, a look of expectancy stranded on her face, a gently "hooked" tilt to her head, posed like a bathing savage atop the pale round smear of her reflection sunk in the maroon pool of the floor.

Outside, between rows of wilting peonies, I hurried down the flagstone walk with the same hot, leaden, hunted feeling I had as when fleeing my father's rest home—a feeling of being closely, urgently cherished by a Predator whose success will have something rapturous about it, even for me.

17

The old man was right; there was a smell about me now. Women sensed it. They flocked to be counselled. The overweight, the underloved, the brutalized, the female brutes. Some were from other congregations; some were unchurched. Perhaps it was that surreal early summer of the Watergate disclosures; everything sure was coming loose, tumbling. My afternoons were flooded with appointments. My phone would ring at the moment I was dozing off at night, and while I was still dreaming in the morning.

What did they say, these women? In sum, that the world men had made no longer fit them. The chafing for some came in the crotch, for others in the head. Some complained that they loved their husbands more than they were loved in turn. Many had the opposite complaint; indeed a curious image of the race of husbands accumulated, as toothless, spineless, monosyllabically vocal, sticky in texture and tiny in size, deaf and blind—the race of axe-wielding percentage-calculating giants who managed the nation became infant monkeys upon entering their front doors. Even the physically violent ones—the strikers, the nightgown-rippers—were described as ultimately docile and so foolable, so obtuse in relation to the essential, as to be figures of manipulation and pity. While many women had had lovers, what remained in their minds was not the male lover's prowess or impact but their own, female, magnificently enclosed suffering. Fearful lest I think them frigid, the women, displaying to me incidents of sexual arousal, admitted, rather than credit men, to curious and neutral stimuli—an infant's sucking at the breast, the moment of an airplane's take-off, the vibration of the dishwasher as they leaned against the sink. Other women, even cinematic images of other women—most notably, that summer, the tartish Maria Schneider of *Last Tango;* Brando was despised for protecting his prick* from the camera—were cited, though very few of my middle-class, Jahweh-worshipping ladies had experienced Lesbian sex. But a vague overarching sisterhood of sensitivity and induced guilt and *not being known* was felt, dawning in most cases as dimly and fragmentarily as the New World dawned for Columbus, a continent in the air; and it seemed

* Prick, pic, truthpic, take it from there, Ms. P.

to me now, watching television, that money, green and golden money which instinctively seeks the light, felt it too, for the commercials, with their invariable feminine heroine, were alone alive, while the sports and "suspense" in between consisted of cursory pap, shovelled out anyhow to male minds of a Merovingian degeneracy.

It generally took four to five interviews to get down to sexual details; the women who came on strong in this respect were most often fronting for some other concern (the death of a parent, the waywardness of a child). When these details emerged, they circled about the business which the younger generation has graced with the unisex term "giving head." Head and heart, tongue and cunt, mouth and cock—what an astonishing variety of tunes were played on this scale of so few notes. Wives who wanted head from their husbands and didn't get it, wives who got it and hated it, wives who didn't mind getting it if they didn't have to give it, wives who loved giving head so much their clitoris indeed did seem to be, like the freckle-faced blue-movie star, at the back of their throats. Somewhere, amid these juxtapositions and their violent "affect," an American mystery was circumscribed, having to do with *knowing,* with acceptance of body by soul, with recovery of some baggage lost in the Atlantic crossing, with some viral thrill at the indignity of incarnation, with some monstrous and gorgeous otherness the female and male genitals meet in one another. I don't know. Perhaps my own willingness, discussed exhaustively above in connection with the underside of church pews, to "go down" was what my troubled women smelled. Or perhaps the traditional sexual ambiguity of the priest, with his swishing robes and his antistoical proclamation of our pain and sickness and sickly need, excited them. For the scoffers are right, ours is indeed a religion of women and slaves.

And I, what did I say, or dare shout, in this gale of female discontent? That marriage is a sacrament and not a contract of convenience. That a spouse, like the land we are born in and the parents we are born unto, is a given; that our task is to love not what might be but what *is* given. That our faith insists, in the most scandalous and ugliest and least credenced phrase of its creed, that we and our bodies are one; that nothing less galvanic than the resurrection of the dead will deliver our spirits to eternity; that therefore, short of physical pain (and anal violation, about which I have a probably political prejudice), we should not heretically (and what a mighty battle the church fathers gave one another over this!) castigate the body and its dark promptings. That our body looks up at us from a cloudy pool; but it is us, our reflection. That the demand for babies isn't what it once was, though evolutional inertia maintains the orgasm as a bribe. That women's rights cannot be established as a symmetrical copy of men's, nor as an inversion of male wrongs.

That communication is often the real problem. That we are all fishers in the dark, in the storm of the senses and mad events, and the tug on the other end of the line must be patiently reeled, with fingertips sensitized by the sandpaper of an abrasive creed. And Heaven knows how much other such not entirely unhelpful stuff.

And I did sleep with a few, by way of being helpful. Fewer, I dare say, than parish rumor or ill-suppressed scandal asserted. But the weeping blotchy-mouthed teenaged bride who had never had an orgasm, and the gaunt divorcee who couldn't stop having them, and the quasi-nun crazy for the liturgy and the Presence and all things dilate with holiness, begged me for a touch, begged though the strength went out of me; and some others seemed, from the description of their private lives, so complimentary to my own secret shape, that we came together as matter-of-factly as two pieces in a jigsaw puzzle. Once the aversion to such use wore off, the church, empty these long afternoons, proved a hushed, capacious treasury of accommodating nooks: the robing room, smelling of clean linen and old paper; the nap mats in the Sunday-school nursery; the ladies' parlor with its Oriental rug and lockable door; my office with its rather sticky and sneeze-inducing horsehair sofa. No partner and I ever tried the nave and its pews; but I was shocked, at first, by how unfussily these seducing women sought out the scrotal concealed in the sacerdotal, how intuitively religious was their view of sex, hasty and improvised though its occasion. Where was their *guilt?* They came to church the next Sunday with clean faces, and listened to the Word intent. There was a continuum for them, where I felt a horrific gap. Bless them all. They brought me out of the wilderness where I did not know that our acts, every one, are homage; only the furniture varies. Churches are spires and domes; we minister now here, now there. There is a grandeur, an onslaught of νοῦς and of dizzying altitude, in the act of placing a communion wafer between the parted lips of a mouth that, earlier in the very week of which this was the Sabbath day, had received one's throbbingly ejaculated seed.

What else did I learn in this unfallow summer of my ministry? That adultery is not one but several species. The adultery of the freshly married is a gaudy-winged disaster, a phoenix with hot ashes, the revelation that one has mischosen, a life-swallowing mistake has been made. Help, help, it is not too late, the babies scarcely know their father, the wedding presents are still unscarred, the mistake can be unmade, another mate can be chosen and the universe as dragon can be slain.* Murders, abductions, and other fantasies flit into newspaper print from the hectic habitat of this species. The adultery of the hopelessly married, the couples in their thirties with slowly growing children and slow-

* But the universe *is* a dragon, as a glance upward into a clear night sky will show.

ly dwindling mortgages, is a more stolid and more domestic creature, a beast of burden truly, for this adultery serves the purpose of rendering tolerable the unalterable. The flirtation at the benefit dance, the lunch invitation stammered from a company phone, the clock-conscious tryst in the noontime motel, the smuggled letters, the pained and sensible break-up—these are rites of marriage, holidays to the harried, yet, touchingly, not often understood as such by the participants, who flog themselves with blame while they haul each other's bodies into place as sandbags against the swamping of their homes. The adultery of those in their forties recovers a certain lightness, a greyhound skittishness and peacock sheen. Children leave; parents die; money descends; nothing is as difficult as it once seemed. Separation arrives by whim (the last dessert dish broken, the final intolerable cigar-burn on the armchair) or marriages are extended by surrender. The race between freedom and exhaustion is decided. And then, in a religious sense, there is no more adultery, as there is none among schoolchildren, or slaves, or the beyond-all-reckoning rich.

Typing this makes me grieve. I fall, full of grit. Generalizations belong to the Devil; particulars to the Lord. Frankie Harlow's pubic bush was copper and curly and infinitely fun to tease. I would tick my eyelashes against it, seeking to sight the horizon of minimal sensation. I would seem among the copper glints to be among stars. She would whisper, far away, and seek to lull me into length. Having failed in her basement, I thought to have her here, in the loft of the parish hall, where a leaking old skylight made vivid the woody forms of miniature crèches and lifesize mangers, wise kings' crowns and shepherds' crooks, Victorian altar furniture and great padded Bibles no longer thumped by the virile muckraking parsons of the first Roosevelt's reign, plywood palm trees and temples of gilded cardboard. We stole velvet cushions from a Gothic deacon's bench and a sheet from a stained-glass window ousted by renovation and made a bower for ourselves. Lovely among the cutouts, plastic, alive, she weakened me with wonder. She was too fine. Shutting my lids on the crystalline curls of her shame, I managed stealthily to approach that apoplectic stiffness that inseminates the world, but when I rescrambled my parcel of bones, skin, and guts so our souls could lock eyes and our genitals do their blunt business, the vision of her skylit face (its pale upper lip an arch of expectation, a gem of moisture set where the crevice between her front teeth met her gum) broke upon my heart with a shining humanity, and manliness went from me. We grieved for me, she wished me to succeed, she loved me the more wildly for my failure; and this wish of hers built firmer the barrier I met in this strange seduction.

And, speaking of seduction, gentle reader, I feel

your attention wandering; Mrs. Harlow's unravished curls rub your sleepy eyes the wrong way. But that barrier barring my satisfying her was, for the terminal season of my distraction, the one living thing in me. I would weep with her, her unfucked belly became a wailing wall, her forgiving hands would stroke the back of my neck, and I would greet my impotence as the survivor within me of faith, a piece of purity amid all this relativistic concupiscence, this plastic modernity, this adulterate industry, this animated death.

I overreach. Swing easy, I tell myself day after day. The days blend here. The sky at night is lilac. The Milky Way is a dragon. I no longer miss leaves. My indignation ebbs. My characters recede. I know you are praying for me, Ms. Prynne.

18

Fall brings with it in those leafy lake-riddled middle sectors of our rectangular land notions of riddance and beginning anew. Alicia's sulk had infected my side long enough. She rebuked me: "Tom, you barged in with 'God be with you' and broke off the Charpentier before it was halfway through!"

"I did?" I was groggy with counselling and resented feedback from my confusion as a middle-aged woman resents the mirror. "There was a silence," I protested.

"It was a two-beat *rest,*" she said, flouncing in her robe, stamping her foot soundlessly on the carpeted aisle. "There was a whole other part of the *Kyrie* to come, with a recorder duet Julie and Sue had worked on for *hours!*"

"Screw," I said, unable in my confused state to resist any semblance of euphony, "Julie and Sue."

"Not them too," Alicia said, making her sour mouth, that recalled to me spoiled sweetness.

I thought this cheap; indeed there was an offensive cheapness to this squat person. Compared to Frankie's silken skin hers was burlap. Her waist was thick; she snuffled. I told her, "I've asked you before, keep the music subliminal. Recorders, trumpet stops, guitars, seven-part Amens, you have it slopping all over the service. Everybody's Sunday roast is charred to a crisp by the time you let us out of your concert."

"Is this you talking, or Mrs. Harlow?"

"Me, thanks."

"Tom. Did it ever occur to you I'm trying to protect you?"

"From what? How?" A tremble of fear waited on her diagnosis; it was indeed diseaselike, her knowing me so well. Our radiant days together had become barium tracers within me.

"By playing so much music. From your making a display of yourself. You're wild these days."

"It's my new evangelical style."

She looked at my chest with glass eyes. "You're heading for a fall, Tom."

"Don't scare me. You sound like my wife."

She blinked, and slightly softened. "That's how we get," she said.

"Who's this we?"

She bit her lips, said, "You know. Us discards,"

and wantonly the wench let her bunny-pink eyes go teary.

Her tears, here in this church (navish tears), displeased me. *Rejoice in the Lord always: and again I say, Rejoice.* I said in a voice of hypocritic honey, "Maybe you'd be happier playing for another church."

She couldn't stop staring, and couldn't stop her inane weeping; in her white robe she seemed a doctor reading the worst from my fluoroscope and choking on the announcement. "May be," was all that Alicia uttered; she pulled her robe over her head and ran down the aisle somehow pulling, in an illusion fostered by my bone-deep fatigue, the entire church after her—rafters, plaques, pews, carpeting, walls, and windows pulled like a printed scarf through the door after her, into the blue outdoors, to her car, a new scarlet Vega. Her old char-dark chariot had chewed up its own transmission and died—fit punishment for all the nights the sight of it, visible evidence of things invisible, had transmitted torment to me.

Ned Bork and I had been creeping together toward an eerie par. His judgments expanded into every area that appeared to me immaterial: he and the secretary* cooked up the church bulletin every

* White-haired Miss Froth; excuse me, I assumed you two had met before. She had your efficiency, Ms. Prynne, but not your heft.

Thursday, he and the youth group held Saturday car-wash parties for the benefit of some North Vietnamese hospital, he was asked by several families to preach the funeral semon* of their departed loved ones, in preference to me. Bork arranged for two families in the parish to adopt black foster children, busloads of ghetto yellers arrived now and then to dabble in our local lake under his apostolic aegis, he was in a court once or twice a week "standing by" some svelte flower child busted for hustling hash or a culturally retrograde beer-oriented lad caught urinating in some policeman's holster. He organized volleyball for the church oddballs and young marrieds (to keep them out of the Oddfellows and Swingers Club respectively) and dominated every game with his bouncy face of hair and his sweatshirt emblazoned (I swear) Jesus Christ Superstar. He organized séances, for all I know. Some salt had appeared in his beard since he had begun to play apprentice to my sorcerer, and even I inwardly registered satisfaction to hear, in his sermons, a diminishment of "you know's" and Jungian protomyths, a growing chumminess of Word and words, a modulation of his preppy drawl into a penetrating nasal enthusiasm that arrowed forth from his mouth our denomination's curare-tipped formulae; in the silence of the congregation, that protoplasmic

* How's that for womb/tomb, life-in-death, etc.? Or maybe I want to say that the corpse, for spurning my steering, is a lemon.

vacuum, I detected a spark or two of unwandered attention from my blank bankers and bakers, a tiny willingness to harken. Ned appeared to them as a new creature. Americans have been conditioned to respect newness, whatever it costs them. Ned's queerness, I also thought, was, in the developing pan of his new confidence, becoming less shadowy, emerging as a faintly fussy and rococo edge for his gestures and dress. It was becoming, really: *potens* was becoming *ens*. My own miserably heterosexual example may have helped him here. Alicia's new car, blood-orange by sulphurous lamplight, appeared at his curb, but not so often, and I imagined them talking, shoeless, through veils of that desexing fumigant called grass. What would they be talking about? Me, I imagined, and dropped into sleep like a shoe.

"Ned, you have a minute?"

"But of course, my rector."

"I mean, I don't want to keep you from going down to the jail and bailing out any of your Jesus freaks for healing without a license." It was better, I thought, that we talk thus; the truth with love, St. Paul prescribes, at a mix of 3-to-1 for normal engines.

Ned's narrow teeth bared on the back wall of his beard. "Nor do I," he smiled, "want to hold you from telling any housewife why she shouldn't murder her husband. Or why she should."

I cleared my throat in the presbyterian manner.

"About Alicia. How do you feel?"

The teeth hid. "She's a friend," Ned said.

I said, "I can see that from my bedroom window. But *intra cathedra,* as an integral part of divine service. Would you raise any objection to our letting her go?"

The preppy fink returned, the clergyman momentarily startled out of his frock. "Why would you can such a dear little blonde bimbo?" His eyes, an intricately notched green, began to flicker as he spun calculations of my sexual politics through his brain, and came up with an answer near enough right to make his flip tone regrettable.

I forgave him it. I said, believing, "She's too much at home behind the altar rail. She'd make every Sunday a Bach fest. I've spoken to her, but the fugues keep tumbling on and on. It's not just me. Others have said so. It's a case of"—and even in the throes of perfidy I had to laugh—"bad vibes."

A dim smile winked in answer. His eyes were undergoing calculations again, and a happy answer shot from them. "If you say so," said Ned. "It's your decision."

"I'd naturally prefer to have it *our* decision. Let's put personal considerations aside. Alicia will survive, she gives lessons, another church will surely take her on, her ex-husband sends her something. Our responsibility here is to the congregation that attends in expectation of hearing the word of God."

He said, only gently evasive, "Actually, I've been at services that have done away with music entirely. You recite poetry instead of singing. There're these great dynamic silences. It can really grab the inner man."

"Quakerism's been done. But I repeat, would you object to our giving Alicia notice? I'll break it to her myself, of course."

"Not really," Ned drawled. "I do think the girl was getting stale." The calculations in his eyes had settled; he offered with a clever diffidence, "If you want to think about another organist, I have a friend you should hear."

"Female?"

"Oh, God, no!" Now my Ned took the initiative laughing; where his beard grew sparse his speckled cheeks flushed with the wine of glee. "Male! A *very* serious person. Unmarried. *V*ery sensitive."

"That sensitive? How does he feel toward the Church?"

"A*dores* it. In matters of doctrine," Ned said, and it was a pleasure to see him so animated, "Donald is con*sid*erably to the right of our Lord and Saviour Jesus Christ!"

"Ned and I have decided to let Alicia go," I told Jane in passing, by way of refectorial offering, as I innocently arose from the lunch she had given me.

We ate when just the two of us at the kitchen table; she turned from the sink, her face intent and white I assumed from contemplation of the porcelain sink, and, the dish she was drying flashing like a shield, advanced toward me with the tread of an army of women. "You're firing her because she slept with you?"

"Not at all. Because she toots her horn too loud. Her sleeping with me is to her credit as far as I'm concerned. But she doesn't do it any more. She's rather like you in that respect."

"Shit," my good wife said, an expression she had picked up from the children, or from feminist talk shows. "I think I'm doing heroically, just to stay under the same roof with you and put a respectable front on all this."

"All this what?"

"All this *you!*" Jane and I never expressed anger. We had suffered incommodities tacitly since the days of noiseless petting above her father's study; I felt her abandoning our married style, and timorously exulted. "It's too much," she was going on, "you just *won't* do that to this woman, Tom. She's over there in that tacky house trying to keep those kids and herself together and you *can't* do this to her."

"Why can't I?" I simply wanted to be told; as I have said, Jane was good, and goodness knows.

But she took it for arguing. Her words came out at a novel pitch, sharped, and speeded, as if she were hurrying messages over a cable about to break. "Because everyone will wonder why and you can't afford that. Because it's an evil careless selfish thing to do. Because there are going to be some very destructive consequences."

"Such as what?"

"Such as *this,*" Jane said, and let fall the plate in her hands; it smashed; from the larger fragments on the linoleum I saw it had been one of Mother's rosy set of Royal Bristol, whose rim pattern of intertwined arabesques I had, during boring grown-up dinners given by my parents, traced and retraced with my eyes until it seemed the very pattern of eternity.

The interview with Alicia was far from painful. Her house, and the afternoon light, had such pleasant associations for me I sang the chime phrase as I rang it and, once inside, stretched in the armchair, overcome by drowsy ease. Her children were not yet home from school. She had greeted me with surprise but led me in willingly; in retrospect I see she might have thought I had repented, I could not live without her, I was leaving Jane. Alicia had been painting the woodwork in the little girl's room. She was wearing denims worn to thinnest blue on each buttock and a man's (whose?) striped shirt with its tail out and a flecked bandana over her hair; she pushed back a stray arc of hair with the back of a hand whose raising released a dove of turpentine scent. She was slow to shed the pleasant harried self-forgetful manner of women working, their grace all unconscious; ah Lord. Each charming second of her deshabille pressed my brain heavier toward the forgetting of my errand. A thick diagonal shaft of dust stood in the room as witness, anxious with Brownian motion. Alicia offered, uncertain, coffee or sherry. In the days, not forgotten, when I came to make love, Portuguese rosé was served in bed. She had wanted to fatten me, the hopelessly lean. I stretched preeningly in my chair, refusing all beverages, and said, "How would you like to get out of your rut?"

"I might like it," Alicia said, perching near me on a footstool, her kneecaps thrusting nearly through the threadbare cloth.

"Have you noticed," I asked, "that you and I seem to be at odds a lot lately?" Above her head (the bandana eclipsing all but a sunstruck rim of her hair) I could see, at an angle flatter than from her bedroom, through her back yard and its clothes pole and blue-hearted birdbath to her garage and an oil truck idling in the alley.

"I *have* noticed," she said, "and I've decided you may be right; I've been too ambitious. I'll go back to Tabernacle Favorites. It'll be less of a strain on me, too."

How wonderfully she was acting the role, of my organist, with the mistress locked inside, breathless to emerge, if I could but produce the winking key. But, "No," I said, "No," drawling it affectedly as my curate, and stretching my legs again in this absurd sleepy ease, "I think your ambition is great, your touch is great, your music is marvellous, and rather than cramp your style I would like to see you hired by another church."

She shifted on the stool, bringing her knees more primly together, but otherwise gave no sign of injury. "You would," she repeated, her mouth tightened into its slightly sideways, gum-chewing set.

"Isn't that good news? You won't have to watch me teasing the congregation any more. You won't have to put up with a preacher so deaf he butts in whenever there's a two-beat rest. You won't be reminded," I ventured in another voice, "of—us."

"I didn't mind that," she said. "I didn't mind being reminded." She brushed back hair from her temple and faced me. "So I'm fired."

"Ned and I agree it would be best for the church."

"Did Ned agree?" She interrupted my contemplated statements about her bonus pay, about the coming weeks of interim. "And the deacons," she asked. "Mustn't they approve?"

Nod. *My* nod, though it seemed to be floating free of me, and got stuck on the ceiling, where I couldn't stop looking at it. "A formality," I said. "At the next meeting."

Alicia stood up. Chin up. Shirt hanging straight from her breasts' bold shelf. I had to stand too, though I had planned to talk on, to speculate about our futures, to reminisce. My body felt heavy, like an old sun. "Thanks, Tom," my hostess said, and I felt her mind moving back to her upstairs painting, "for telling me yourself. For not putting it into a letter or over the telephone."

I thought she meant this sincerely. I thought it *had* been good of me to come and risk a scene that, praise God, had not transpired. I was as full of illusions as a sunbeam of dust. I wondered if it would be remiss of me not to attempt to kiss her good-bye. Nothing in her stance invited it, so I said instead, stooping (at our old partings she had always been above me), "You *do* see that it's a blessing in disguise, don't you?"

"I'm sure I will," she said, "though right now"—her smile was encouraging—"I can't stop seeing the disguise."

Beyond her shoulder lay a faded loop rug; I wanted to curl up on her warm floor like a cat. Did I make an attempt to? In memory she seems to lift a hand as if to hold me upright. "Just go, Tom. Don't say any more. I'll manage."

Or some such. As I stepped into the outdoors, which was by contrast chill as lake water, her door snapped behind me (locked?) and I felt a premonitory disorientation, like a fairgoer whose wallet has been picked from his hip pocket but who, at first, only subconsciously misses the comradely backpat of its weight.

19

We thought a motel might help. All August Frankie had been with her family in some dank resort northward, playing tether ball and canoeing amid lugubrious pines, feeding mosquitoes on the nectar in her veins, admiring Harlow's dragonlike skill at igniting brickets. September was distracted by the return of children to school, October by my flurry with Alicia, and anyway the old happiness diet of narthex necking and sneak sexual snacks had become starvation rations with this new, intimidatingly exquisite love. We needed time if not eternity. We cobbled up a tryst for around All Saints' Day. Since even out of town my face might be recognized (by a buried man's mourner, by a Sunday school student matured, by a renegade Friar Tuck who might hail me from some ecumenical banquet past), Frankie did the distasteful business with the register and the key; she emerged from the red-blinking OF-

FICE (ORIFICE, I kept reading it as) in her good cloth coat as cool as emergent from matins, having tipped the collection plate. She took the driver's seat of her car (my drab Dart adrift in the twinkling tin sea of a shopping-center parking lot) and drove the little distance, a short chip shot (keep those wrists *stiff!*) to the door with our number on it. Scuttle, scuttle, and don't forget the paper bag containing our lunch, *vin,* and plastic forks and spoons, picnic in the shade, bucolic customs revisited.

The room was unlike this one in accidents rather than essence. Indeed the increment of profit from the tribute we paid then and of the vast drafts of Christian charity supporting my holiday here may eventually trickle to a single bank account, just as a drizzle in Pittsburgh and a flash flood in Casper mingle droplets in the New Orleans delta. The room had a big bed, a bright bathroom, an empty bureau or two, thick curtains that could be drawn, a wastebasket to catch our tangerine peels, a mirror to catch our skins. We had everything; we were as astronauts; we were more than the world.

Frankie, in one of those spatial delusions to which I had been lately prey, seemed to fill our chamber with her delicacy as a spider fills a corner with filaments; she moved here and there, bestowed bags paper and hand, disposed foldingly of her cloth coat, disclosed a black dress so simple and stylish and perfectly chosen for its few moments of motel wear that I wanted to weep, unsnapping it and peeling its softness up, save that it was too early for me to weep, my impotence had yet to be demonstrated. Her high-heeled black shoes, her stockinged feet with their heels flat on the carpet (so childish for all their shapeliness, and childish the pressure of her hands on my head for support as I tugged the smart shoes off; the years dodged away between me and the time when girls at grammar school had pulled my hair, when I had hair, when there was recess, and licorice belts, and paper snowmen glued to the windows, and nobody told us that Jesus had not *really* been born the day after a snowstorm), her feet then bare, bared by my reaching up to her waist to tug down the tights that, so transparent upon her, darkened to a black puddle from which her feet stepped gleaming, every bone a jewel, the toes a stung little pink: lovely, she was lovely at every stage of undress, I could have stopped anywhere and had a creature of paradise, she had so considerately dressed herself for my undressing, lovely in her dress, lovely without it, lovely in the fine-beaten necklace and bracelets and the wristwatch she removed without my asking, lovely even the almost-boy without her bra but still in pants, a topless *mignonette* adequately attired for the beach at St. Tropez, and, these pants (enhanced with a ribbon of ruffle and a floral weave of watermark delicacy) flippingly shed, lovely in only her fleece and fingernails.

She stood amused, looking over her shoulder at

herself in the mirror, waiting for me and my move. More roughly undressing myself, I realized her air, tentative and considerate, of dealing with something fragile, did not have to do with herself and her nakedness, which only my awe lifted out of the ordinary for her, but with me, whether even in this perfect and purchased seclusion I could break through her skein of glory and, in the human way, screw her. And my sensing of this doubt swelled my qualm to its familiar insurmountable dimension.

We lay together, played together, made light of each other; I caressed her and let myself be caressed and finally, my bit part stubbornly shying from the role of hero, gave her a climax with my face between her thighs. How tigressishly, how self-forgetfully, she pushed for those last, breakthrough beats! I was pleased. We ate. The wine had already been half-consumed. Our stolen hours were dwindling. I sought to explain myself.

"I can only think," I said, "it has something to do with your being such a staunch churchwoman."

"But—" She delicately halted.

"The others are too? Jane and Alicia? Jane doesn't believe in God, she believes in the Right Thing. Alicia even less. She likes music and men and that's all she has the spiritual budget for."

"And am I," Frankie asked, shedding shyness, "the only other—?"

"Not exactly." The melancholy and muffled one-shots behind the choir robes I did not want to betray, even to her. Right of therapeutic privacy. "But even if the woman *is* a church member, she doesn't embody faith like you do. You seem really hipped on it. The way you used to look up at me through your veil."

"I'm not veiled now," she precisely said, and bit a Butter Nutter cookie with her smile. "And *am* I" —speaking crumbs, one hand cupped beneath her chin to catch them, lest they make the sheets hurt— "so hipped on it?"

"I think so. Do you believe in God the Father Almighty, maker of Heaven and Earth?"

She blushed and, her voice as modest as possible, answered, "Yes." A fury gathered within me, an amateur plumber's frustrated rage at being unable to dissolve my lump and unclog my ability, my after all hideously common and as they say God-given ability, to deliver myself into this loved woman's loins.

"Say you don't," I commanded.

Frankie didn't understand.

"Say you don't believe in God. Say you think God is an old Israeli fart. Say it."

She wanted to, she even took breath into her lungs to utter something, but couldn't.

Easy stages, I thought. "Say 'fart.' " She did. I gave her more words to say. She passed them through her lips obediently, untastingly, like a child in catechetical class. The corners of her lips curved, pronouncing; she was amused. Our litany excited me; she noticed this, and moved to capitalize; at a new angle I admired the sequence of her vertebrae and the symmetrical flats of her winglike scapulae; I pushed her off, and brought her face up to the level of mine, and held it so hard her cheekbones whitened and her eyes went round. "*How* can you believe, Frankie? How can any sane person?"

"Many do," she told me. Then amended, "Some do."

"It's *so* ridiculous," I said. "It's always been ridiculous. There was this dreadful tribal chauvinism of the Jews. Then some young megalomaniac came along and said, Look at Me. And about a dozen people did. And then . . . We don't know what happened, nobody knows, all we know is that as the Roman Empire went rotten one mystery cult prevailed over the many others. People were as messy then as they are now—it could have been any cult. And the damn thing's still among us. It's an establishment, Frankie love. A racket. Believe me. The words are empty. The bread is just bread. The biggest sales force in the world selling empty calories—Jesus Christ. What is it, Frankie? A detergent? A deodorant? What does it do, Frankie? This invisible odorless thing."

"It lets people live?" The feel of her fragile small jaw struggling to move under my fingers was exciting. My grip had tightened the fine wrinkles from her face.

"It lets them die," I corrected. "It likes them to

die. This summer among many delightful distractions I watched a fifteen-year-old boy die of leukemia. He was an ordinary boy, a little duller than most; he couldn't understand why him, and I couldn't either. But he was old enough and bright enough to know what a meaningless foul trick it was; why don't you? Suppose it had been Julie? She's fifteen now, isn't she? Suppose she's struck by a car, while we lie here? How would you feel?"

"Terrible. Sinful." Her eyes, though watering with pain, still searched my face for what I wanted, so she could give it.

I dropped my hands to her throat. A fasces of veins, pumping. I asked her, "If a demon were to enter me and make me strangle you, do you think God would stop it?"

"No." She was frightened, yet tittered; my sudden touch had tickled.

I hit her. First a tap with a cupped hand, then really a hit, with open palm and stiff wrist so our chamber split at the noise, and all the gossamer threads her love had spun were swept away. "You dumb cunt," I said, "how can you be so dumb as to believe in God the Father, God the Son, and God the Holy Ghost? Tell me you really don't. Tell me, so I can fuck you. Tell me you know down deep there's nothing. The dead stink, Frankie; for a while they stink and then they're just bones and then there's not even that. Forever and ever. Isn't that so? Say it."

"I can't."

"Why not, sweet? Why not? Please." I got to my knees and crouched above her, I wanted to lift her away, to safety, away from myself. Paradoxically, I suppose.

"I can't," she cried under me, lightly twisting.

I brushed away the hair agitation had tossed into her eyes. "Why can't you? You know there's nothing. Tell me there's nothing. Tell me it's a fraud, I'm a fraud, it's all right, there's just us and we'll die, there's just your dear cunt, just your dear ass, your tits, your dear mouth, your dear, dear eyes." I touched her eyelids and thought of pressing down.

She bit her lower lip rather than speak.

I crouched lower, urging, clowning. "There is Noboboddy, Frankie, with his faithful dog Nada. There must be nothing. You can't think there's a God. You know you can't. What's your reason? Give me one reason, Frankie."

"You," she said, in a voice half-hostile, and this hostility brought her soul so close I moaned and bowed my head to take my gaze from hers; I saw my own phallus erect up to my navel. She spread her legs quickly, but not quickly enough, for though I entered her, repentant tenderness overtook me; her pelvic bone gnashed against mine as I melted inside her; she came, wide to whatever was, while I couldn't, and it became my time to weep again. She pulled my face down to hers, so roughly I resisted; she thirstily kissed my tears.

"Forgive me," I of course said, "I don't know what happens to me. But at least it was something for you, this time, wasn't it?"

She nodded tremulously, still lapping my tears; her tongue felt so large and strong and single I remembered the kiss when her mouth had seemed to have many petals. She formed words. "You must think of this," she told me, "as holy too."

I rolled from her, her fair body sunk in a trough of sweat. The fresh air on my skin reconstituted the world. "O.K.," I said. "That's good practical theology. I'll try. I think I'll get there next time."

And events did not prove me a false prophet. There was no next time. Distilling my ministry, I find this single flaw: Frankie Harlow never did get to feel my seed inside her, sparkling and burning like a pinch of salt.

I hurried up the brick walk fearful that my motel adventure had consumed more time than even a deathbed might explain away; I need not have worried. In my absence the world had moved beyond any demand for my lies. Ned was there, with Jane; they were sitting in the living-room, in the easy chairs opposing each other by the fireplace, as often when I returned from a night errand in the errant era when I had hoped they might fall in love. Only now there was no fire in the fireplace, the weak daylight of an autumn suppertime bleached romantic shadows from the stage set, and both were sober.

As I entered the room, passing beneath the oaken archway with its divinely worked tympanum (cruel as a guillotine if it fell) of knobs and spindles, they both stood, absurdly in unison. I feared the boys might overhear whatever they would say; but from the far end of the house sounded the electric sloshing of television's swill.

Jane glanced at Ned and took a step forward to speak. "Tom, Alicia—"

"Didn't like being canned," Ned interposed, achieving, with a springier step than Jane's, a parallel position on the rug. "So—" He respectfully nodded toward my better half.

"So she went to Gerry Harlow's bank and told him all she knew."

"Which was evidently quite an earful," Ned said, drawling in his vile old style.

After waiting for me to respond, Jane went on, endearingly pained, her forehead looking skinned and her mouth so taut it seemed out of sync, "Not just about you and her, but about—"

"You and everybody," Ned finished, his lustrous beard curling in a thousand smiles.

Jane said, "He was here, for an hour this afternoon, very upset—evidently Frankie wasn't at home or anywhere—and is calling for a meeting of the deacons at his home tonight."

"Very hush-hush," Ned said.

"He of course wants it kept as quiet as possible, a

sudden vacation, say, we could say a nervous breakdown or whatever they call it now—"

"Gerry called our good bishop," said Ned, "who told him there was a place even, out West, for cases like yours; evidently cases like yours are the coming thing."

My bishop: a brick-red man in black sitting in a brick-red city rimmed with black industry. To him I was a black pinhead on a map of Christian services—filling stations, refineries, sales offices—within the region. *Prick,* I could be moved. I felt tiny in his eyes and stereoptically huge, a pallid monstrosity beyond the pale, in these two gazes, Ned's warmed by a not unfriendly froggy-green satisfaction, Jane's cooled by goodness and pity and a hopeless blue sense of distance. Without a witness there she would have run into my sooty arms and homogenized with me into one gray one. Ned's presence saved her this. They were waiting for me to speak.

I laughed and asked, "Why do you two remind me of a pair of hi-fi speakers?"

A waste of a question, since they couldn't help it, they were a pair, my instinct had been right, a matched pair of prigs.

20

O, Lord.

Another Sunday is upon us.

Our text shall be taken from Deuteronomy, the thirty-second book: "He found him in a desert place."

Moses is speaking of Jacob, but it might well be of himself, or of a dozen other of the God-chosen men of the Old Testament. The verse continues, if failing memory serves, "He found him in a desert land, and in the waste howling wilderness; he led him about, he instructed him, he kept him as the apple of his eye."

I would propose, my dear brethren, who have deserted the world and been deserted by it, to meditate this morning not upon the loathsome Old Testament God, His vengeful plagues and pestilences and His preposterous obsession with circumcision and with His own name, nor upon those enigmatic brutes, such as Moses and David and Samson, upon whom His favor incorrigibly and unlodgeably rests; but upon the desert, the wilderness as it is more often called, that encircles the world of Bible as parched sand girdles an oasis and bitter black space surrounds our genial and hazy planet.

Though the drama of the Bible is islanded by history, the wilderness is always there, pre-existent and enduring Adam and Eve are sent forth from their disobedience into it, and our Lord Jesus at the dawn of His ministry retired unto it, to be tempted of Satan. There, as Mark with his characteristic pungence tells us, He "was with the wild beasts; and the angels ministered unto Him." And for each of the forty days of His fast and vigil there, the children of Israel wandered a year of their forty in the wilderness of Sin, or Zĭn, or Sinai, wh[illegible] their thirst was often keen, so keen that o[illegible] one occasion the Lord left off His fearsome chiding of His children and led Moses to the Rock of Horeb, and bid him smite, "which turned the rock into a standing water, the flint into a fountain of waters." Our soul, the Psalmist says, *thirsteth* for God—Whose doctrine, we are told elsewhere, drops as the rain, "as the small rain upon the tender herb, and as the showers upon the grass." "He leadeth me beside the still waters; He restoreth my soul"—the special world of God within the Bible is an oasis world; the world beyond, the world of the Lord's wider creation, is a desert.

Now we dwell within the desert. Its air, clean and sweet as mythical ether, astounds our faces as we emerge from the shelter of this benign hostel; we see, on the golf course, the frantic sprinklers doing a dervish dance to keep the heartbeat of green alive; lifting our eyes to the hills, or accompanying our excellent Ms. Prynne on one of her well-shepherded nature walks, we confront a cosmos of fragile silica, rock flaky with long baking and inhospitable as a stove-top to the touch. Seeming lakes prove mirages of shimmer, or else gleaming *playas* paved with salt, not the answer to thirst's prayer but its very mockery. For all the taming clichés of tourism and frequentation that a gross and frivolous empire can impose, but a few quick steps from the beaten path, into the solitude beneath a red rock, serve to convince us that this grandeur is heedless; its breath is a dragon's, its innumerable eyes are blind. Gratefully we return to our haven of cool and shade, and sport in the swimming pool whose water, pumped from deep in the parched earth as greedily as the Bushman in the Kalahari sucks life from the sand through a straw, draws upon the precarious water table and subtly causes the desert to extend itself elsewhere.

For the desert is growing, make no mistake. Pastoral man is more predaceous than the pelted hunter. Entire herdsman nations in Northern Africa have been grazed to desert, where famine now reigns. Many a green landscape where our Saviour walked, and Eden itself, and civilization's very seedbed in Sumeria, have become blanched valleys, home to none but the sheeted Arab. According to geologists, there is more desert now than at any era in the earth's billions of years. Utah was once all a lake. Dinosaurs waded through swamps where now lizards skitter across the boulders of their petrified bones.

And in other senses as well is not the desert also growing? The pavements of our cities are deserted, emptied by fear. In the median strips of our highways, naught blows but trash. In our monotonous suburbs houses space themselves as evenly as creosote bushes, whose roots poison the earth around. The White House itself, intended by its builders to be the center of probity and the symbol of candor, seems instead a burrow wherefrom the scorpion of falsehood emerges only to sting, and sting again, again, and to hide as before.

In the parish hearts it was once our vocation, brethren, to safeguard and nurture, did we not feel a frightful desert, of infertile apathy, of withering scorn, of—to use a strange Greek word suddenly commonplace—*anorexia,* the antithesis of appetite? These barbaric Biblical heroes whom Jahweh appointed the apple of His eye—what sins did they not commit, save this one? Virile bridegrooms lusty for the world, where are they now? Is not even faithlessness, which once assaulted our piety with the vigor of a purer piety, now a desert beyond reclamation, a feeble and featureless wilderness where none but the most degenerate of demonic superstitions—astrology, augury, Hinduism—spring up in the hearts of the young, until they too soon cease to be young, and nurture in their blasted greenness not even these poor occult weeds? What has our technology, that boasted its intention to reconstruct paradise, shown itself to be but an insidious spreader of poisons? Where has it landed us, as its triumph and emblem, but upon the most absolute desert of all, the lunar surface where not even a lichen or a microbe lives?

And yet, and yet . . . For those of us whose heads God has turned, so our very collars are shaped like a pivot, there must always be an "and yet." And yet, how gratefully our lungs inhale this thin desert air! How full, to the acclimated vision, is this landscape devoid of buildings and forests! How luminous the rare rain! How precious the sparse cactus-flowers!

We all know the name Death Valley. How many of us have heard of *La Palma de la Mano de Dios?* So the Spaniards called the harshest basin of the American desert as they knew it. The Palm of God's Hand. Are we not all here, in the palm of God's hand? And do we not see, around us (with the knowledgeable guidance of our dear Ms. Prynne), the Joshua tree lifting its arms awkwardly in prayer, and hear the organ-pipe cactus thundering its transcendent hymn? What a chorale of praise floats free from the invisible teeming of desert life—the peccary and the ocelot, the horned lizard and the blacktailed jack rabbit, the kangaroo rat that needs never to drink water and the century plant that blooms but once in decades. How ingenious and penetrant is life! Living-stone cactuses mimic the stones they push between, whip snakes toss themselves from bush to bush, the mesquite plant can send taproots down a hundred feet, the ocotillo tree sheds its leaves to minimize evaporation and continues photosynthesis through the green of its bark. Birds nest in thorns. Tiny pupfish, transformed from the piscine inhabitants of the once-vast lakes, survive in the salt-saturated pools that remain. More wondrous still, tadpole shrimp hatch, grow, mate, and die all in the few hours of a flash-flood puddle's duration, and with their dried corpses leave eggs to hatch when the next puddle appears in that place many years in the future. The seeds of desert plants wait cunningly; a mere sprinkling does not tempt them to breach their carapaces; only an acid-stirring deluge dissolves. And then the desert is carpeted with primroses and poppies and mallows and zinnias, and the tiny ground daisy and the desert five-spot and sand mat and rock gilia entrust their miniature petals to the glare of the sun, and the Mariposa lily remembers itself, and the sticky yucca blossom invites the yucca moth, and the night-blooming cereus its lunar brother, and the tiny claret-cup cactus holds up its cup to drink. And when the king of the desert dies—when dies the great saguaro cactus—it leaves like a man a skeleton, its soft flesh falling from the woody ribs that held erect its fifteen tons of nobility.

What lesson might we draw from this undaunted profusion? The lesson speaks itself. Live. Live, brothers, though there be naught but shame and failure to furnish forth your living. To those of you who have lost your place, I say that the elf owl makes a home in the pulp of a saguaro. To those upon whom recent events still beat down mercilessly, I say that the coyote waits out the day in the shade. To those who find no faith within themselves, I say no seed is so dry it does not hold the code of life within it, and that except a corn of wheat fall into the ground and die, it abideth alone; but if it die, it bringeth forth much fruit. Blessed, blessed are the poor in spirit.

Brothers, we have come to a tight place. Let us be, then, as the chuckwalla, who, when threatened, *runs* to a tight place, to a crevice in the burning rock of the desert. Once there, does he shrink in shame? No! He puffs himself up, inflates his self to more than half its normal size, and fills that crevice as the living soul fills the living body, and cannot be dislodged by the talon or fang of any enemy.

We *are* found in a desert place.

We *are* in God's palm.

We *are* the apple of His eye.

Let us be grateful *here,* and here rejoice. Amen.

21

Do I detect an extra whiteness, as of erasure, in the blank space beneath the conclusion of yesterday's sermon? Holding the suspicious spot up to the light, do I not espy the faint linear impress of a pencilled word? There seems to be a capital "N," in a pedestrian school hand—can the word be "Nice"? Ideal Reader, can it be you? If the word was "Nice," why the naughty erasure, the negative second thought, the niggardly Indian-giving? But bless you, whoever you are, if you are, for this even so tentative intrusion into these pages' solipsism, this pale smudge fainter than the other galaxy that flirts with the naked eye in the constellation of Andromeda.

Three weeks ago today I was put aboard the silver bird, the chariot of fire, that brought me here, by a little windblown party of Jane, my two sons, and Ned—windblown for mid-November had come to our green flat land, and the airport was flatter than flat, so that even the first drifts of snow, thin and bitter as crusts of salt on a dead lake's shore, had no rest, but undulated and scuttled against our hurrying shoes, and my witnesses had no shelter from the whirlwind of my translation. Stephen was crying because of puzzlement, and Martin because he had overheard and understood a bit too much, and Jane because weeping was a wife's right thing, and Ned because of the wind.

Frankie and I had managed our tears (and even here, I could scarcely come, so forgetful of grief did her perfection render me; my ducts barely squeezed forth a drop of ichor each against the pressure of her tailoring and the shimmer of the Corrèges scarf mauve at the throat of her chalkstripe suit and the nicety of her gray-gloved hands, hands whose naked ghosts haunted the bower of our pleached memories—her hands being shoved testily into her pockets of mink in my office, her hand with its moist palm leading me by one of mine into her basement, her lovely hand caressing my limpness, her alert hand cupped to catch crumbs from her mouth in the motel) at some narrow coffee nook in the city we were suburban to. I faltered, "The first time we kissed, you had given me coffee."

"It gives me the shakes," she said.

"Gerry really doesn't know?"

She shook her head silently; her own tears had

found, on the glaze of her cheeks, fine channels to follow.

I said, counselling to the end, "Maybe you should tell him. You can't rebuild on sand. On lies."

Frankie, sitting proper across the little Formica table, which was snow-white and ice-slick and held within it a pink blur that was her face reflected, leaned forward an inch and pronounced distinctly, in that garden of a voice whose far corner was shaded by magnolia, words of an alarming vehemence. "I don't want to rebuild, I want to destroy. Everything but us. I don't want that bullying simpleton wallowing around in what you and I had."

"We didn't have much," I pointed out. "I don't mean *you,* of course, I mean—"

She knew what I meant; her gloved hand waved it away. "It would have happened, and been beautiful," my dear devotee avowed.

"Don't destroy," I begged. "You have so much. The house, the furniture—" Perhaps my solicitude for her furniture induced that smile of fine slyness detectable behind her veil—no, she had no veil. Like my reverence for her furniture, a slip. "Think of Julie," I said.

She lifted her wide gray eyes—wide as the local horizon is wide, too wide to be taken in all at once, which is disorienting, which may explain . . . but never mind. As when she had come to me to complain about Alicia's music, her tone seemed alarmed. She said, "I'd come with you, you know."

"You can't. You mustn't. I wouldn't let you. You stay here." Accustomed to ambiguity from me, she lowered her face as if slapped. Then I tried to make myself cry, with the weak results you know.

Alicia stayed unseen in the embarrassed week between her revelation and my departure. She needn't have; the very vulgar thoroughgoingness of this her second betrayal—as contrasted with the wistful muddle of her first—had a happy liberating effect upon me; for until now I had not quite yielded up the hope that she would take me back, on an idle afternoon, into her bed, with its quilted sunburst. It would have been so easy for her, and easy for me, to be rejoined to that triumphant lazy body she called forth from the crypt of my daily existence. Now that she had repaid me in full for my treachery (that is, for my staying with Jane and the cloth and the parsonage), I was quits with my guilt and my hope. Whatever guilt there was, she could shoulder.

Ah, I seem, in that lost vineland, to take the stance of a haughty white hunter who wishes to stroll into the jungle with his hands unburdened; the life I have sorrily described is as a departure point at which I am busy hiring various women as porters for the great train of guilt that is my baggage. Jane carried a load for not adoring me as would a mistress or Mary Magdalene; Frankie bore some for adoring me so much I became with her a desexed angel; and now Alicia, toward whom I had felt heavy for failing to make her my wife when she was so much my woman (see earlier etymology), took on her head the bulky bundle—the struck tent—of my collapsed career. Well, she was thick-waisted and tough and could tote it. Babies and guilt, women are built for lugging.

Time had ceased for my father; whether I was away a month or an hour was the same to him; I was a recurrent apparition that tripped a circuit in his brain. "Ras the rascal," he hailed me fondly, "still up to his mischief. When was it you dipped Lena Horsman's thick braid in the ink well and she shook her head so it spattered across the linen shirt our mother had mended for Sunday wear? Laugh! If ever there was justice done; she told us how you took her dog fashion, *comme lès chiens*, her little *derrière* upthrust for demonstration like a double helping of *glace vanille*, eh? Ah, well, we can't be saints all the time, the Lord would get bored. It was a vomitous crossing, and I dread the one back."

"Daddy, please try to listen to what I'm saying."

He looked at me with terrifying minuscule eyes. "What do *you* care," he said, his indignation beginning, "about the capital of Bangladesh? What's it to you, if Bebe Rebozo has a real name? This false hilarity amid so many appliances, whom do you think it fools? I asked for clean walls and a view of the lake, and you give me indecencies in charcoal and curtains drawn tighter than a bear trap. I know some call it art. I call it blasphemy and insubordination; I have a right to my power tools." He leaned forward so anxiously his great woolly head jerked, and I feared it might roll from his shoulders. With these confidences came from his mouth a meaty scent of the lunch he has just consumed. "I have a son," he told me, "whose duty it is to incarcerate fools like you."

"Daddy, *I* am your son. It's me, Tommy. They're sending me away. They say I've disgraced the ministry."

His little eyes blinked as if singed, and seemed to clear. "Well, no doubt you have," he said wearily, in a voice that fit the moment, that had abandoned the effort of filling its many other spheres. "No doubt your mother's blood, it had to tell. She was a tart, you know. I wept to control her, I tried reason and passion, faith and works, but she needed more of the world's goods and pleasure than I could supply, so she turned from my bed to you and your indolent friends, steeped in the muck of inherited wealth."

"No," I pleaded, desperate to hold him to reality, my reality, that only he could forgive. "I am your son. Something's gone wrong. I have no faith. Or, rather, I have faith, but it doesn't seem to apply."

He heard my cry and inside his hollow head

struggled to keep his mind from sliding away. "I gave her," he explained to me slowly, his voice doubting the words but unable to frame better, "what comfort I could. Had you not appeared, she would have been contented enough."

He was apologizing to me; I seized this hint of a bond. "What shall we *do,"* I asked, "to keep her with us?" I touched his hand, his ancient mole-mottled hand with mine, that was more lightly mottled, and becoming ancient. His skin was cold. "Daddy, I'm frightened. Tell me what to do. What shall I become? I wanted to become better than *you."*

"There's none of that," he said, his voice having entered some sixth realm, beyond indignation; and the thought went through me chillingly—not a brain-thought, but a blood-thought—that he would not live till my return. His hand slid from under mine and got on top of it, and patted absentmindedly. "There's none of that," he reassured me, "until we get to be a little older."

At the airport I abruptly squatted down and took my two boys, so quickly they could not shy away, one in each arm. To Martin I said, holding tighter as his wiry body tensed, perhaps angry with me from what he understood of my flight, "Be nice to your brother while I'm away. And take it easy on yourself." To Stephen I said, "Don't get too turned on by anything." His still babyish face looked puzzled and disappointed; I tried to explain. "Don't listen to the radio instead of doing homework. Don't argue with your brother more than you must. When I come back I want you to tell me your month has been hassle-free." And I let them go, and stood up, and kissed Jane. She was pale, and there was a little crust, but it broke through, like a thin mirror breaking, and there was nothing to say, as when one is alone.

Nice?

22

Well, another interview from that tiger cage of a claustrophobic week returns to me. Dimly. Too many shimmering cactoid days, too many 8-irons drifting just to the right of the green, too many inside straights that didn't quite fill have intervened. Gerry Harlow came to my office in the church. Our official interview, the one with him barking ultimatums that packed the combined clout of the deaconage and the bishopric (he didn't bark, to be honest; he "issued" them, through clenched teeth or, more exactly still, out of a close-shaved jaw whose masseters kept bulging), had taken place in the parsonage, the night after the night after my motel afternoon. This was days later.

This was different. He wanted something. I had been cleaning up my desk, so Ned as acting minister could have some drawers. I motioned Harlow into the counsellee's chair and sat down myself. He looked like a man who had been out in a wind too long; his face had a sensitive high glaze and in the chair he leaned forward, his lips stretched back from his teeth like a skier on a tight turn. He hoped, as a starter, that I understood he had been acting as a spokesman of the church and parish, rather than in any private capacity.

I said, Of course. I said I had admired his efficiency and clarity of purpose.

There was more stiff and manly palaver. I was glad I was not applying for a loan. This fellow knew how to wear authority's spacesuit. I thought of Frankie's skin against his and felt her shiver. He had the astronaut's lingo, too. Most of Alicia's allegations had "checked out." (The teenaged bride, especially, had been cheerfully circumstantial, as if her episode with me had been a TV episode she were redescribing. But even the gaunt divorcee had, off-handedly, confessed. As I have preached in these pages, women really don't see much wrong with it. Indeed I was grateful to Harlow for putting me back in touch with some negative directives, from male mission control center.) Since, he said, I had consented to be launched into a leave-of-absence, this "operation" was a "closed book" for the time being as far as he was concerned.

I reeled out six or eight seconds' worth of silence.

But, he said, one thing, frankly, was bothering "the hell" out of him. Harlow deliberated a micro-second over the "hell," but then calculated that, reverend or not, in view of his data, I could take it. The thing was this: Alicia had at first incriminated among the others his own wife, Frankie (as if I didn't know her name. As if orderly procedure dictated we begin from utter scratch). When, Harlow said, he had come back to it in their conversation, Alicia had shied away, became vague, said it was just a guess.

I asked, "What does your wife say about it?"

The wind he was in burned his face a shade pinker. "She denies it."

"You doubt her denial?"

He said, effortfully groping for the truth, he who in his business of giving or withholding loans customarily had the truth neatly pre-stored in the bond box behind his grimace, "The very flatness of it feels wrong—taunting, brazen even. It's as if she doesn't want me to believe her, to be satisfied. It's as if—she hates me."

"Oh no." The promptness of my response was suspect, and odd, considering that she had several times told me just that. But my feminine side quailed at the thought that this provider of the expensive, new, glassy, giant-sized furniture Frankie lived among could be hated. This was her living lord. I said, "In her sessions with me I received very few unambivalent signals that that was the case, though she *is,* and you must know this, at a stage in her life where she should become reacquainted with her own needs, after all these years of other-directed activity—the others of course being primarily yourself and your children." Besides Julie, slender recorder-playing Julie, there was a boy, Barry, a thirteen-year-old copy of his father, odiously successful at school, a precocious mocker in the choir, a savvy little shark of a boy, a bankling in bud.

Gerry Harlow said, "A neighbor woman told me she saw you coming out of the house one day."

This accusatory fact took me aback, my masculine ego was so effaced in the Christian effort of soothing his doubt and saving his marriage. A witty out occurred to me: "That must have been Jane in slacks," I said. "We look alike, you know."

His answer came straight from space: "Tell me another."

Adopting his metallic tone, I told him then, "There's no reason you should take my word, except that this week you will have noticed I haven't denied anything, and have nothing to lose at this particular point in time. Right?"

"Right."

"So to you I swear, solemnly, that I never"—the word had to be exact—"fucked your good wife."

He waited his judicious second; then a bolt shot back in his brain, his grimace unlocked, his lips retracted, the gold caps of his molars gleamed. I had the loan. He said, "Still, you know her in a way I don't; she's talked freely to you."

How condescending! I had put on skirts in his eyes. I had asked to; yet now itched to tell him the truth, the sexual acts that *had* been, her shameless, slavish acolytism. I said nothing.

He went on, relaxed, winding up details, "What shall I do with her? Should I give her the gate? She kind of wants it, but aside from the children, I'd hate to do it, she's so damn presentable. And we knew each other when. With some other person, you don't have that." I realized that the "neighbor woman" who volunteered her glimpse of me to him must have had a reason, and an occasion, to do so. So not even chairmen of boards of deacons were spared the plague, our Dance of Death. He finished. "On the other hand, I don't want to waste the rest of my tour with a woman who hates my guts. There's something of the nun in Frankie, always has been; she can be hard."

I sighed. My desk top, now bare of my papers, my pictures, my paperweights, heaved slightly, as it did on the edge of exhaustion, or when I pondered it preparatory to counselling. "From the little I know of the two of you," I told Harlow, "you are *married*. She's discovered she can say the worst of what she feels and the world does not come to an end. She'll calm down. Who else does she have, but you? Whatever she makes or imagines of some other man or of freedom itself, they are not *serious*, compared to you. She knows this. She is a Christian; she knows where the center is. You are the center. Let her resolve around you, no matter how far out she swings. Love her, listen to her. She loves you—by which I mean merely that you have gravity, and the rest of us don't."

I realized that, in my weariness, I had half-belied, in this final phrase, my carefully framed innocence; but then realized, from the something fervid and conspiratorial and painful in Harlow's parting handclasp, that he had accepted my profession as a technicality, that Frankie had certainly betrayed to him her love for me, that he had been after not an absolution but a working basis, and he had it, and was thanking me. And I felt, sealed by this comradely handshake, a consignment and betrayal of his wife; I had sold her to her husband, when she had begged for flight, for release from gravity, and decency, and duty. It was my duty so to do. How sad I felt, seeing Harlow leave, his shoulders square as those of a young soldier who has just acquitted himself well with an ingenious and more than her trade demands affectionate whore.

Gerry, Frankie, Julie, Barry—how small remoteness has whittled them. They seem dolls I can play with, putting them now in this, now in that obscene position. I put the Frankie doll in a nightie, and lie her in bed, and spread her jointed legs, and set the Gerry doll on top, while the Julie and Barry dolls sleep the dreamless sleep of the safe and the inorganic. I look down upon the copulating dolls by removing a section of the roof no bigger than a chessboard. The Frankie doll's painted eyes stare up at me blindly. I am too big to see. Is it impossible, ideal and severely tested readeress, that by entering this giant square state, from my smaller busier one, I became a giant, among giant dogs and clouds and saguaros; that even letters in the mail sack, crossing the state border, swell into our scale, and that ominous knock beneath my feet in the 707, which for a dip of my heart I took to be the commencement of an inescapable dive, was merely the notch of our transposition, my quantum-jump birth as a Titan?

Ms. Prynne, on behalf of all us boys of this peculiar Boys' Town, I want to thank you for the tour yesterday of the dinosaur-bone quarry. The bus trip was most fun, what with the singing and the pranks, but the arrival itself had something of its intended educational impact. Who would have thought the matrix was harder than the bones themselves, and that the process is like drilling away the tooth to leave the filling free. And the scramble of those huge bones!—as hard to decipher as the spaghetti of motive and emotion heaped in our hearts!

Grains of sand, one by one, make an aeon in the end. Yet the solemn and insupportably vast prospect of time opening from the panorama window of these fossils was smudged by the noisy activity of young paleontologists wearing laboratory frocks over jeans. A dime held close to the eye eclipses the sun. No matter in how many ways our lives are demonstrated to be insignificant, we can only live them as if they were not. To the friable thecodont phalanges and the distorted bone crest of the corythosaurus, let me add in the interests of science some bones extricated from this sedimental narrative:

Alicia's patellae thrusting palely, edgily forward when she sat on the arm of the church pew and, again, when she sat on the stool in her living-room.

Frankie's scapulae glinting when in the motel she offered to go down on me.

Ned's humerus, which I momentarily seized in the parsonage yare.*

Gerry's mandible tensing and untensing in my office.

Jane's pubis grinding on mine above her father in his study. ("Let my bones be bedewed with Thy love," I seem to recall from one of St. Augustine's more excited perorations [Pusey translation].)

My father's skull, greater and stranger-brained than a baluchithere's.

My elder son's backbone (figurative).

My own troublesome and mortal "bone," which comes and goes. As what does not, eh Ms. Prynne? O you are the matrix of us all; grain by grain you bring us down, and rightly scoff at the thunder of skyey bluffers such as me.

* My first slip in a week of Sundays. My yard of yore?

23

Did not sleep well last night. Homeward thoughts within me burning already? The first week, I slept hardly at all, it seemed; I laid down my head inside a lonely plastic droning that was proceeding west at 550 miles per hour, at a cruising altitude of 34,000 feet. Then, grain by grain, this place stopped moving, it became a *place,* and now the danger is it has become the *only* place. And this accounting the only accounting, and you my reader my only love.

Let me tell you a few golf stories. In the first week of my stay, when the contours of the course had not been sprinkled brightly into my brain (I have been thinking a lot about love, these days, my hatred of the word, my constant recurrence to it, and it occurs to me, one of insomnia's perishable revelations, that before we love something we must make a kind of replica of it, a memory-body of glimpses and moments, which then replaces its external, rather drab existence with a constellatory internalization, oversimplified and highly portable and in the end impervious to reality's crude strip-mining), I played alone, the front nine, as my companions went in to their rooms, their pills, their remorses, and their naps, and on the seventh, as the immense bandshell of desert sky was resonating with muted lilac on one side of the orchestra and on the other side a pink pizzicato of cloud-stipple was tiptoeing toward the cymbal-clash of a fiery sunset (hang on, it's my therapy, not yours), I came down off the hill with a solid but pushed drive and, from an awkward lie, a 5-iron that, in the way of the unexpectedly well-hit shot, went over the flagstick pure and skipped off the green. You remember, of course, how the apron on this side is a little shoulder, glazed on top by a spiked hardpan that invites a scuffed shot every time. But a power greater than myself with my own hands took a 7-iron from the bag, pictured the chip crisply, swung crisply, and watched the ball hop from the clubhead; it jiggled over some worm-castings (the greens committee flies the worms in from Brazil at great expense), hit the pin with a heavenly *thunk*, and dropped in. A birdie three. Joy, for almost the first time since I had beheld Frankie's foot bare on the motel carpeting, unweighted my heart. The next hole, of course, is that very short par-three, a mere 120 yards by the card; I took an 8-iron, and with a relaxed little poke pictured the ball a-glint by the flagstick. Instead I saw it flutter sideways into the impenetrable shoulder of sage and creosote bush on the right. And *the next shot went the same way*. A brand-new Titlist. I scored myself an X on the hole and dragged back to the clubhouse. My face felt scorched; I had encountered the devil. I had brushed up against a terrible truth: it's the sure shots that do us in.

Or, to put the moral in a more useful form, even a half-hit demands a shoulder-turn.

And a full intention: lukewarm I spit thee out.

Golf is as it were all bones, an instant chastener and teacher; lessons glow through, shapely as the graphs of binomial equations, that would hide forever amid the muffling muscle of lived life's muddle.

Here is a more human story, and happier for your hero. Last week we were in our usual foursome—me, Jamie Ray, Amos, and Woody. Woody and I had on our usual dollar Nassau, and as usual he was outdriving me by fifteen yards. I don't see how he ever got those shoulders into a cassock, and don't wonder the Vatican decided he needed a cooling-off. Every time he thinks about the Latin Mass his face goes red as a lobster and his claws begin to rattle. He got Jamie Ray as partner today, which meant he was sure to collect on the team play. Jamie Ray swings miserably but putts like an angel; I sometimes wonder if buggery hasn't made the hole look relatively huge to him. Whereas us poor cunt men keep sliding off to the side, hunched over fearful as fetuses who suddenly realize they can never push their craniums through a three-and-a-half-inch pelvic opening. Amos must have been a rapist once, for he tries to hit the back of the cup so hard a miss (and most are) runs two or three yards past. I know, of course, dear directress, that Amos's crisis was asexual. We've all spilled our beans, though forbidden to. He was the pastor of a happy little outer-inner-city church, wooden colonial, all pillar and pew, annual budget around twenty thou, two hundred families on the rolls, maybe fifty active. A cheerfully dying little situation, no strain on a man of sixty, head bald as an onion, arthritis creeping into the joints, children off in Teheran and Caracas working for the government or the oil companies, an arthritic evangelical faith kept a little limber by the sprinkling of blacks in the flock and a lot of civic busywork in the "community at large." Suddenly, the church burns down. Faulty wiring? Panther-Muslim vandals from the ghetto one neighborhood away? A loose Jovebolt? No matter, in a great rally of solidarity and if-God-be-on-our-sidism they voted to rebuild, and did, a spiffyish little altar-in-the-round job of cream-colored pressed-garbage bricks, shaped like a hatbox with a hatpin pointing out and upwards. The only trouble was, no one came. The blacks thought the money should have gone into community action, the old faithfuls couldn't stand the new architecture, the younger element took to tripping in one another's basements and calling it devotions, and the rich family that had principally contributed never came anyway, having lived here when this outer-inner city was working pasture at the end of the trolley tracks and still believing that the religious duties of a squirearchy were fully absolved by a Christmastide appearance. Amos's wife and Korean foster-child attended services, and some of the local teenagers who thought they were possessed would break in nights and do things on the altar that left damp spots, and the volleyball and yoga groups thrived upstairs; but it wasn't enough for Amos. The emptiness, the silence, the mortgage payments, the shoddy workmanship and materials of the new building, the funny smell when it rained—they got to him. His custodian found him one Saturday night in the furnace room soaking newspapers in kerosene, and here he is among us.

But you know that story, and I began to tell another. Golf. Golf, gold, goods, gods, nods, *nous,* gnus, anus, Amos. Eight strokes, with some cheating and a one-putt. Amos's golf had the peculiarity that, no matter with what club he struck the ball, from driver to wedge, the arc was the same—low and skulled-looking. But he was straight, and could be depended upon for a customary bogey, leaving me free (free! a word to be put into the stocks along with *love:* one an anarchist, the other a fornicator) to go for the pars. Still, against a hot putter and a big hitter, what hope was there? Precious little. A saving remnant. Woody had me three holes up with four to go. On the fifteenth he hooked his drive into the pond. *"Unum baptisma in remissionem peccatorum,"* I said to him, and drove short with an iron for a safe five. Three left and two down. A comfortable cushion, his shoulders implied, my little banderilla of Latin quivering as yet unfelt. Or perhaps felt as an unneeded surge of divine afflatus, for he overswung his fairway wood on the spacious sixteenth fairway and topped it badly; it scuttered into a prairie dog burrow. At least, it vanished, in that band of scruff bordering the arroyo. The four of us circled for ten minutes, like old women gathering fuel in vacant lots you might say, before giving up. *"Qui tollis peccata mundi,"* I consoled my priestly opponent, and complacently (I confess it) chipped my own, indifferent but safe wood shot onto the green, for another winning bogey. Jamie Ray had run into trouble in a bunker, and Amos found the dead center of the back of the cup, so we saved some quarters on the team debt as well. Woody felt the world sliding; as we teed up for the par-three seventeenth, I beheld descend upon him for the first time the possibility that his lead might dissolve entirely. He was rattled; he was excited; the Latin had tripped open sluices of *excessus* in him. He surprised me unpleasantly by popping a 6-iron onto the dead center of the green, which slopes toward the sunset, California, and the Sea of Peace that bulges toward the infinite like an unblinkered eyeball. My own 5-iron took a lucky kick and seemed against the glare to creep onto the right edge of the green. Neither were Amos nor Jamie Ray in trouble. Hosannah.

One must walk down steps of orange shale here. The light was so nice, our evening drinks were so close, our match was so amusing—slung among us loosely like a happy infant in a blanket we each held a corner of—that we talked loudly in our joy, and once on the green I, the first to putt, lifted my arms and incanted, *"Pleni sunt coeli et terra gloria tua."* You may or may not be surprised to know, my ms.terious Ms., that they have licensed me as the clown of the group.

Nothing clownish, however, I pictured the line of my long putt so firmly it became a Platonic Ideal in my mind, as hyperreal as a cubic inch of Sirius would be on Earth, in the second before its weight collapsed the examining table and burned a tidy square tunnel straight to China; and I stroked it, and, while it did not go into the cup, it trailed in close enough for a gimme, which is pretty fair from fifty feet. Woody, ruddy with the sunset glow and the remembrance of the Mass spoken as God meant it to be, not unpredictably powered his fifteen-foot putt half as many feet past on the downhill side, and in sudden consternation putted short coming back, and took a squandered four to my struggled three. One to go, and all even. Our friends were amazed. I was a miracle-worker even if I lost.

And of course I did not. Pure, floating, purged of all dross, my swing drove the ball a sobbing seventh of a mile toward the edge of the sun; Woody, pressing but not destroyed, was one swale shorter, but straight. He hit (Amos and Jamie Ray poking along beside us like men pushing peanuts with their nose) first, and a cloud momentarily muted my sense of transcendence as I saw that his shot was a beautiful thing, hitting behind the pin so hot it backed up. Yet, out of love for you, Ms. Prynne, among others, I took a 7-iron and gazed from the height of my compact and unhurried backswing at the ball on its crystalline plane of sparkling sand and grass until more suddenly than a melted snowflake it vanished. My divot leaped, which they don't usually do. For a professed lover of down (being, going, staying) I have an odd resistance to *hitting* down; I can't believe the ball will rise of itself. I can't believe the world will go on spinning without me. I can't believe any woman will be happy without me. I can't believe I am not really fifteen billion light-years in diameter and shaped like a saddle, etc.

I let my head lift. Oh, with what a sublime comet's curve was that shot bending gently in, from the half-set sun's edge to the tilted flagstick. I lost the ball in the shimmer of the green, but my glad bones guessed it was inside his. And so it was. Our walking revealed the balls in a line with the cup, his ten feet past, mine five feet short. And still the priestly devil, the minion of the Babylonian mother of harlots, gave battle. His putt, stroked with a Jesuitical fineness, broke away at the last mini-second, as his ally the snivelling Dixie pederast grunted. Whereas my problematical five-footer, too confidently stroked from within my trance of certain grace, would have slid by on the high side had not a benign warp of the divine transparence deflected it; it teetered around half the hole's circumference, but the eventual glottal rattle, there could be no denying. My partner, stout Amos, applauded. My opponent looked at me webbily, through the crazed windshield of his shattered faith. *"O salutaris hostia,"* I saluted him, and felt myself irradiated by the Lordly joy of having defeated—nay, crushed, obliterated—a foe.

Tomorrow we would all be resurrected, and play again.

24

Again, trouble going to sleep, and fitful waking, between dreams designed and fumbled together by some apprentice subconscious. The body gets into these habits. The bed stretches beneath me tense as a trampoline. I am preparing for some leap. The backwards version of the leap that brought me here?

Yet I like flight; I like the food that is brought without asking, from behind; I like the tinkle of the serving dolly drawing closer, one's saliva tinkling in response; and the giant hum, and the nursery blues and greens of the plastic decor, and the nation's checkered midriff unrolling below. Nothing to do but observe and endure. Between worlds we are free. In *la palma de la mano de Dios.*

It occurs to me that at least three times before in these enforced confessions have I discovered myself above, exalted, *raptus,* looking down as at the golf ball ere smiting it so triumphantly into the heart of the eighteenth green. Once, when returning from a nocturnal mission of mercy to find Ned and Jane fumbling in boozy friendliness beside my fire. Twice, when serving communion to a kneeling recent fellatrice from the height of my priestly role. Thrice, looking down, in my overarching embodiment as author, through the lifted roof at the Harlows' domestic bliss, their house and its inhabitants reduced by reminiscence to a doll-sized seizability. So, perhaps these moments of naked megalojoy show the true face of my grovelling, my comical wriggle in the mud of humiliation. What is a masochist but a sadist whom weakness confines to empathetic satisfactions? And vice versa—the Marquis himself, a careful reading reveals, only wanted to munch excrement in peace. Concentration camp inmates imitated the dress and manner of their SS guards. Captives of pain, all; captives of one category. Freud's darkest truism: opposites are one. Light holds within it the possibility of dark. God is the Devil, dreadfully enough. I, I am all, I am God enthroned on the only ego that exists for me; and I am dust, and like the taste. What is all this reduction I have described, my defrocking myself of dignity, righteousness, respectability, fatherhood, husbandhood, even of an adulterer's furtive pride of performance, but a form of exaltation, an active reaction within a fixed vertical tube? Even my defeat of Woody: is not the heart of its joy nothingness, the nothingness that the annihilator experiences on behalf of the annihilated?

Something crucial in all this, but it skinned away from me as one of your Apache chambermaids went rattling down the hall, humming some fetching snatch of popular electronics. A fetching snatch herself, no doubt.

Did you like yesterday's word golf? Let's play again, let's see if we can get from "love" to "free," those two subversive words so dear to deluded Americans. Love, fove (Webster's preferred spelling for fauve, meaning a tawny beast), foee (an expression of contempt), free. Only three deft shots, a birdie! The words are the same underneath, and free love not a scandal but a tautology.

Transparency. My unseeable theme. The way a golf swing reveals more of a man than decades of mutual conversation. Woody's hearty grunting lunge and the disarmed delicacy of his short shots, which bobble to a premature stop on the apron; Amos's freckled bald head twitching its invariable six inches leftwards as his skulled ball rockets on its defused arc toward a quick reunion with the ground; slithering ashamed little Jamie Ray's redeeming mastery on the greens, the way he tucks his right hip back and tucks his right elbow into it and the back of his gloved left hand moves along toward the hole like a floating guardian above the clubhead and the way his dingy narrow face turns with the follow-through as if he is peeking underneath a porch and then is split by the beginning of a smile as his ball, halfway there, bends knowingly toward the hole, which brims with expectancy, a cup that drinks—we men are spirits naked to one another, on the golf course we move through one another like fish a-swim in one another's veins.

What we know, we move through; it is not opaque; nor an obstacle; nor an enemy; it is us, yet not us. Panovsky points out that the Age of Faith proclaimed *manifestatio,* in its scholastic argumentation and in the visible articulation of its cathedrals. The cross-section of the nave can be read off from the façade, the organization of the structural system from a cross-section of one pier. My father's carpentry opened the furniture of my childhood to me and made it religious; the women who came to me as dark bundles and resistant tangles became transparent in being fucked. I know them; one cannot know and not love.* In this sense the Greeks were not so naïve, in supposing that to know the good was to do the good.

By knowing, we dissolve the world enough to move through it freely. We dispel claustrophobia. Think of the auto mechanic, how greasily graceful his sequential descent into the problem, as opposed to the dumbo (me) who thumps the hood angrily upon the obdurate puzzle of his non-starting engine,

* Know, enow, 'nuff, luff.

and crushes his thumb. By knowing, we dissolve the veneer our animal murk puts upon things, and empathize with God's workmanship.

True of the pathologist who descends daily into the scribbled microforms of malfunction and disease?

True of the pearl-diver who scrapes his breathing-hose and drowns amid the billion lives of coral?

And, worse, isn't there something demonic in such dissolution; can it be the devil urging us into wider and wider transparency, where we no longer see to marvel, and feel nothing but the sticky filaments of our analysis, and have a Void where there had once been a Creation?

Dear Tillich, that great amorous jellyfish, whose faith was a recession of beyonds with these two flecks in one or another pane: a sense of the world as "theonomous," and a sense of something "unconditional" within the mind. Kant's saving ledge pared finer than a fingernail. Better Barth, who gives us opacity triumphant, and bids us adore; we do adore, what we also love in the world is its residue of resistance—these motel walls that hold us to this solitude, the woman who resists being rolled over, who is *herself*.

Ms. Prynne, forgive me, I seem to be preaching out of season. I do apologize. As you have seen I am not only a sinner but a somewhat cheerful one, though my clown's costume has been reduced to tatters. A clown, moreover, capable of cruelty, at least toward that side of me in bondage to decency; I have been cruel to Jane.

Doing right is, to too great an extent, a matter of details, of tinkering. That great gush of heavenly *excessus* runs dry in a desert of rivulet distinctions. When is it right for a man to leave his wife? When the sum of his denied life overtops the calculated loss of the children, the grandparents if surviving, the dog, and the dogged *ux.*, known as Fido, residual in himself. When is a war good to fight? When Pearl Harbor is attacked. When does an empire begin to die? When its privileged citizens begin to disdain war. Ethics is plumbing, necessary but dingy. Ethical passion the hobgoblin of trivial minds. What interests us is not the good but the godly. Not living well but living forever.

I distrust these assertions, though I seem to believe them. Truth more likely to grow from small hard perceptions, dicotyledonous in form: the pairing of carpentry and lovemaking, for instance. The musky smell of shavings, the ecstatic *ratio* of disassembly, the concentration among flung limbs, the need for a bench or a bed to work upon, the joiner's pride when it all comes together.

Ms. Prynne, am I trying to seduce you? Help me.

My love of my fellow golfers has helped me to understand Alicia, her flirtations, her many lovers. To be a woman among men is to be surrounded by sexual pressure; the lightest touch invites, the smallest submission releases. The pressing of a key, the pulling of a stop; and what eager tones, what a hungry wind of power! She was making music with us that only she could hear. She was organist, church, and congregation. How superb, to be a woman! At moments, in the bar afterwards, I let the rank maleness of my fellows blow through me, and try to think their wrinkled whiskery jowls, their acrid aromas, their urgent and bad-breathed banalities, into some kind of Stendhalian crystallization. I cannot quite do it, I am less than half queer. But love these fools, tough as I am. And to be a woman, what a constant pleasurable outpouring of forgiveness it must be, to be so surrounded! Like the sensation of sweating on a bonny summer day.

Once I was startled by a glimpse of male beauty. I drove to a school to pick up a sixteen-year-old boy. As he ducked out of the entryway, having spotted my car, he flicked his hair, which continued to bounce as, taller than I remembered him, he loped down the steps; I was seeing him with an unusual perspective, as a young male in the world, severed from me. He was, suddenly, quite without intending it, beautiful. He was my son Martin.

Amos brought a Polaroid along and took photos of us on the eleventh tee one day. I am plainly aware of being photographed, yet also trying honestly to hit the ball. I have just hit it. My head is trying to stay down, though the swing is completed. I see, laughably, the left knee locked, the right foot still illicitly harboring some weight, the arms badly collapsed, my belly, navel showing, thrust with an odd one-eyed earnestness toward the unseen fairway. As I remember, the shot was a massive slice that led to a six. There is a bank of cactus and mesquite behind me, a wedge of sharply shadowed rock above, a triangle of sky. At my feet the horseshoe-shaped tee-markers, and the maddening rubber driving mat, and the confetti of broken tees. I feel in the distance at which I view myself, holding this snapshot, Amos holding the camera, and feel outside the rectangle of the print the silence of our two playing partners, waiting and watching. I see, not quite in focus, a middle-aged, quasi-mesomorphic clergyman doing an ungainly but solemn imitation of an athlete, beneath an alien desert sun, amid the trappings of vacation, in a moment innocuous and lost. I want to laugh, but my throat locks, dried by the realization that this is a picture of me in Paradise.

25

Poker takes a larger group, seven and not always the same seven. Woody plays, but the money makes Amos upset, and Jamie Ray prefers the more finesseful microcosm of bridge. Myself, though I hadn't played since college and had to learn the rules of the baroque variations introduced mostly, among us poker-addicted parsons, by Fred, the only minister I have ever met who stutters, and remarkable also for his exhaustively red hair—apricot color on his scalp, bright chestnut in his eyebrows, a washed-out almost custard shade in his lashes. He has a loud voice, stutter and all, and loves to bet. He always gives the pot a kick, he never lets the flywheel of us rest. And I have not been able to discover, without seeming to gossip or pry, what he is here for or what his denomination is.

The transparency of poker of course differs from the pellucid swings and distances of golf: we skate directly upon the glassy surface of the Lord and his dispensations. The encounter, indeed, at first was too turbulent and dizzying, too charged, not only with the psychologies of my fellow-players but with the irrefutable whims of the Bestower of Gifts Himself; so that I, in the dizziness of which beer was a component, became rattled. Being rattled takes two forms: betting losers and folding winners, in boustrophedonic alternation. But, glory be, one's fellows, knowing you to be rattleable, are loathe to fold against you, where a steadier player would convince them, and they would thriftily steal away. So some of the losses return, given that one (as one must, in a mathematically random universe) has the cards sometimes. Thinking you a fool, they do not believe; they stay, and you reap. Credence, so abstract and tenuous in real life, becomes bread and butter in poker. Also, as in international relations, a curious indeterminacy principle obtains: a margin of unpredictability must be maintained around you. So the stupid act becomes obligatory if one is to have a *presence*. When I emerged from my rattled first nights and found I had a poker presence, it was as heartening as discovering, with Alicia, that I had a sexual presence. I have settled to winning some and losing some, trying to keep a card count, trying to curb my Thomistic optimism—give me two fours and in jubilant certainty that the other pair will arrive as a *donum superadditum* I raise. Thus our hero sits on his hardened haunches at an octagonal table from nine to twelve every night in a blissful stupor of Desert Rat Beer and as it were origami eschatology (clitoral eschatology, I want to say, God knows why, something about the way the corners of a deck thrill when rippled), watching the breath of the Lord play across the surface of the cards and the faces and the fortunes of his new-found friends.

Want to hear a poker story, Ms. Prynne? It must be good for you; just as one excursion into the girls' room (no urinals!) is good for every American lad. We were playing a game called Eighty-five. You are dealt five cards, the first face down; then you can buy three, one at a time, each after a round of betting, discarding every time. It is a high-low game: the best possible low is Ace, 2, 3, 4, and 6 of not the same suit. Same suit would be a flush, Ace-2-3-4-5 would be a straight; both high; get it? Though Ace can count as 1 it also tops the King and a pair of Aces is the highest pair. Fred was dealer; I sat to his right. By the third "buy" card the other hands had either folded or were on the face of it committed to going high. I had showing Ace, 2, 4, and 6: a super low, patently. The trouble was, my 6 was paired underneath. The one hand left to draw, Fred's, was nondescript garbage, Jack high. Intuition told me he too was paired. Nevertheless, to be safe, thinking I at least could do better than a pair of 6's low, I threw the down card and drew—*oof*—an Ace, giving me a pair of Aces. Providence had really stretched to discomfort me, for the other two

Aces were on the board. Fred, announcing "D-d-d-dealer will take a c-c-card," threw his Jack and got an 8. Not a bad low, now, but mine looked so strong I felt sure I could drive him out. I raised; he raised me back. I raised again, figuring he had been testing, and would fold now. He did not. The third time, then, but with a sinking heart, I raised, and he raised back, which with the raising among the highs (four cards of a flush against a possible full house) made quite a leafy pot. The betting done, I called low, as did Fred, and told him, "Damn you. I'm paired."

"How h-h-h-high?" he asked.

"Aces," I confessed, wondering why he asked.

He had the worst low possible for his hand showing, a pair of eights. Fred had stayed, then, against me when only one card in the deck, the cased Ace, could have made my hand a loser to his. Two truths dawned upon me:

He was crazy.

He had won.

He had raised not on a reasonable faith but on a virtual impossibility; and he had been right. "Y-y-y-you d-didn't feel to me like you h-h-h-h-had it," he told me, raking in.

And I felt his craziness in him like a glowing tumor I longed to touch and heal; I wanted to reach into him, as into a great red-haired chasm, and finger this pulsing marvel of the craziness that made him stay against odds worse than those of Pascal's notorious bet.

I wanted, that is, to minister unto him.

And unto these others; imperceptibly these errant and bankrupt clergymen have replaced the phantoms that chased me here, phantoms it now seems my heart had conjured from its own fevers, had bred like fungi in an unlit dank of self-absorption. This desert sun has baked them away. This desert sun has reduced old bodies to their bones, and given me instead these shaken, hearty, boyish, mortal ministers. In these last days I have heard myself listening to Amos and the tale of his expensive empty church, and advising him that this emptiness is itself eloquent, and a Word, if he but believe that God is not a pathetic dwindling old gentleman but an omnipotence that moves and creates everywhere, that "potently does everything in everything," in the words of Luther, who hailed God's power even in the Turks and Vandals—competing street gangs, it turns out, in Amos's neighborhood. The Church was never meant to be a quantitative success; Christianity is not an industry in competition with other industries. Amos, and so many other colleagues broken and stranded by the ebbing of faith, seem to me racked upon Calvin's curious transition from the absolute majesty and remoteness of God to the possibility that cleverness and thrift in the management of capital is an earthly sign of divine election. It has made our American faith brittle. It has made it crass. Amos's job is to stand and witness, not to pack a room, or operate a "plant." So I try to tell him, with jokes and an implicit fondness.

Woody's rage for Latin, his rage against the bishops and the Berrigans and all who have polluted and distorted and abandoned the sacred fixed forms of the one true faith, I try to suffer in such a way as to bring to his own ears, in the silence of my attention, an echo of undue bitterness, a hint of indignation misplaced from a more personal fear of obsolescence, perhaps a hierarchical envy, an unspeakable suspicion that if such surface adjustments as a translation into the vernacular and the dismissal of St. Christopher and the marriage of some Jesuits can occasion so massive a "falling away," then what was fallen away from had long died, was its husk only, a husk of goldleaf. Woody believes everything because he believes nothing and his anger is terror and his terror is lack of faith.

And to Jamie Ray I have listened even more intently, though smiling at his delicious Southernisms ("asshole slicker than a buttercup" comes to me out of many) and rejecting the sidling fear that any announced homosexual puts into me, trying to detect, for myself and for him, what holy thing it is men see in each other, what fear brings them to cling only to their own sex, though their bodies become, not manly, but mockeries, often fanatically skillful, of the despised feminine. What deep comment on our condition, our ambiguous soul in its palatial but deteriorating prison, is being made here? It seems almost sane, but for an undercurrent of predation and brutality—the use, for instance, of the still sensorily innocent and dumb bodies of boys. What is, old Professor Chillingworth asked through me, the good here mistakenly aspired to? That the mistake occurs deeper than the conscious will, I of course implied to Jamie Ray, and he knew I admired his putting, and he my mid-irons, and so we became a bit less opaque to one another, fumbling and shrugging. I told Jamie Ray, giving myself the pleasure of confession, how, in my despair and bewilderment at being unable to fuck Frankie, I prayed God for the power to have an erection; I begged Him to be my accomplice in adultery, and believe that, had not events intervened, the prayer would have been answered. Our God is a fertility god.

Fred, too, sensing my vivid glimpse of his craziness, and my marvelling at it, has become more relaxed with me, and stutters less.

It is hard, of course, to console or advise professional consolers and advisers; rote phrases, professional sympathy, even an emphatic patience are brusquely shunted aside. At a convention of masseurs no one turns his back. So we learn to say nothing as a way of saying it all. The stately desert silence sets us our example.

As the silence is infecting me, and driving me to short paragraphs.

You ask, what of my own case? A common fall, mine, into the abysmal perplexity of the American female. I feel, however, not merely fallen, but possessed, and such is demonology that the case needs for cure another woman; and the only woman here, on this frontier, is, Ms., you.

26

Aven* less sleep than the night before. A churning to get something done. A genuine fear of the return to the world. My left palm tingles, thinking of it; my body at night lies transposed into a graver key; the existential solemnity of my unique ego and fate is borne in upon me as sweatily as death by plague. My defiantly tricksome style of earlier has fallen from me; I limp, lame and fuzzy-brained, from one dim thought to the next.

Spent an hour now rereading, between winces of embarrassment, the pages we (you and I, reader; without you there would be the non-noise of a tree crashing in the inhuman forest) have accumulated. Not, you say, a very edifying or conclusive narra-

* And a return of auspicious misfingerings. This one hard to read—was going to begin with "Again"? A longing for haven. A half-hope of heaven?

tive. A man publicly pledged to goodness and fidelity scorns his wife, betrays one mistress, is ompotent* with another, exploits the trust and unhappiness of some who come to him for guidance, regards his father and his sons as menacing foreign objects, and through it all evinces no distinct guilt but rather a sort of scrabbling restiveness, a sense of events as a field of rubble in which he is empowered to search for some mysterious treasure.

How much, I see backwards, has been left out, even in the zealous matter of sexual detail. The startling hardness of the teenaged bride's breasts, for instance, and the uncomfortable way she liked to have them entirely in my mouth, so my old jaws ached. And the gaunt divorcee, her pubic bush the only bump on her, in profile outthrust like the jaunty pompon of a poodle. Whereas Frankie's hair lay in flat neat circlets, so flat and neat they almost seemed painted on her belly's supple parchment. And many other such details that might have lent plausibility and morally suasive substance to my furtive display of smuggled icons.

Nor is the end clear. I do not expect to find my parish there for me when I return. Ned is in charge; the androgynous homogenizing liberals of the world

* Dear me. My suggestion of omnipotence in impotence reminds me of Meister Eckhardt, with his cyclical assertions that Everything is God, that all things merge so that everything is nothing, that God is nothing. The triumphant atheism of mysticism. Give me Thomistic degrees instead. There is *something*, dammit. Damn It?

are in charge, and our American empire obligingly subsides to demonstrate how right they are. The East, the dust between the stars, will prevail. Alicia I do not expect to be there; Ned for his own fey reasons will not have reinstated her, my firing will stick, my plumping for the Word as against pretty liturgy. My last Barthian act. Alicia, I see now, was like those brimming golden afternoons of boyhood, that yet we do not wish to live again, because we do not wish to be again the pint-size, allergy-ridden, powerless person who enjoyed them.

Frankie and Jane are less clear. I aspire within both women as, in some surreal and stippled Doré print, a faunish sufferer struggles to rise within a translucent hellish chute of intricate folds and bannister-like turns. The one all ethics, the other all faith, and I between. No. The formulation does the reality a disservice; there is something gritty, practical, mortised, functional in our lives, something olfactory and mute, which eludes our minds' binomial formulations. I can scarcely believe that either woman waits for me. It is as if the overpopulated green land I left has been blasted to desert by the process that has filled this bare place for me with habits and pleasures, affections and names and flowers of interest.

And yet . . . It is a few minutes to noon. A golf game waits, yet not with the innocence and air of abundant escape it had before I wrote days ago those pages bringing it and my companions (not, I fear, entirely convincingly; altruism still tickles my sinuses with a fearful must of futility) into this garbled and saddening audit. In a few days I will leave them. It will be cold at home. My father will greet me under another name, and my children will ask for their presents. Jane—her face is blank. Frankie has moved away, her love for me self-satisfying, self-contemplating, love in love with love.

Last night, dizzy and headsick after a game of poker unrelievedly boring in revenge for my morning's attempt to describe its fascination, I stepped out of this omega-shaped shelter, testing my impending freedom, and looked up at the stars, so close and warmly blue in this atmosphere, yet so immutably fixed in their dome of night; and I felt, for an instant—as if for an instant the earth's revolution had become palpable—that particle or quantity within myself, beyond mind, that makes me a stranger here, in this universe. A quantity no greater than a degree's amount of arc, yet vivid, and mine, my treasure.

God, the sadness of Creation! Is it ours, or Thine?

27

My brothers: our text today is taken from that Prince of Preachers, the one born out of due time, Saul of Tarsus who became Saint Paul, his epistle to the Corinthians, the fifteenth chapter: "We are of all men most miserable."

We? Who is this we? We who preach the risen Christ: "And if Christ be not risen, then is our preaching vain, and your faith is also vain."

Your? Who is this you? You of Corinth who profess the monstrous new faith, who have received the Gospel, the good news derived from the reports that the dead man Jesus, risen from the tomb, was seen by Cephas, and then of the twelve, and after that of five hundred brethren at once, of whom—Paul says, in that haunting aside that gives this epistle the breath of contemporaneity, the diaphanous urgency of yesterday's newspaper—"the greater part remain unto this present, but some are fallen asleep."

And now all are fallen asleep, and have long been so. Still to this day late in 1973 the rumor lives, that something mitigating has occurred, as if just yesterday, to align, like a magnet passing underneath a paper heaped with filings, the shards of our confusion, our covetousness, our trespasses upon the confusions of others, our sleepless terror and walking corruption. "So when this corruptible shall have put on incorruption, and this mortal shall have put on immortality, then shall be brought to pass the saying that is written, Death is swallowed up in victory."

When? Something has not yet happened. Paul expected it to happen soon: "Behold, I show you a mystery; we shall not all sleep, but we shall all be changed, in a moment, in the twinkling of an eye, at the last trump." The last trump did not sound before Paul slept, nor has it in the long centuries since, centuries crowded with appetite and battle, with lust sowing lives even faster than disease could harvest them, centuries each of which is like a chalice brimming with human tears and blood lifted in homage and oblation to the God above appeal.

Yet still men listen for that last trump; just yesterday, on the delightful bus trip to Sandstone arranged by our capable Ms. Prynne, to prepare us for re-entry into the world, and to buy our children and our wives leathery souvenirs, a tall and gracious youth, the very image of a youthful Jesus save that Jesus was no doubt historically darker and shorter, a third-worlder to his filthy fingernails—this youth handed me a pamphlet illustrated with cartoons of Richard Nixon collapsed beneath a "Shield of Incredibility" and with intricate diagrams of the Sun's perihelion and the comet Kahoutek's orbit in relation to the November ceasefire and the Winter equinox; this pamphlet, produced in Dallas and repulsive in its crazed computations and slangy piety, predicts the end of the world in eighty days, and makes much of the unBiblical slogan, "Around the World in Eighty Days."

May I share with you a paragraph of this cretinous prophecy?

"You see what Jesus show me? Isn't that wonderful how God shows His people! Begins the 12th (November), day after the *Peace, peace* and then on (January) 31st with war, war! Savvy?—And sudden destruction! You in the *U.S.* have only until *January* to get *out* of the States before some kind of disaster, destruction of judgment of God is to fall because of America's wickedness!"

Well, we recoil from this gibberish, with its devilish savor of astrology and drugged radicalism; but let us ask ourselves, is not the content of this miserable throwaway, promulgated by the most desperate inanity of a desperately inane generation, is not the content, as distinct from the style, the content of our life's call and our heart's deepest pledge?

Consider, again, another pamphlet, pressed upon me by the same weedy Jesus, who singled me out from the giggling pack of you as the one most conspicuously in need of redemption. Under odious purple illustrations, and in a coarse printing aimed at the puerile, we find this travesty of the epic mystery of the Atonement: "God is our great father in Heaven and we are his children on Earth. We've all been naughty and deserve a spanking, haven't we? *But Jesus, our big brother,* loved us and the Father so much that he knew the spanking would hurt us both, so he offered to take it for us!"

Well, even so: yet have we listened to our own Sunday school teachers, or our own singsong children's sermons? Is not our distaste here aesthetic, where aesthetics are an infernal category; is not our love of Christianity an antiquarian and elitist cherishing, a dark and arcane swank, where a living faith for the lowly should obtain? Does not this pornography of faith, like the pornography of copulation printed in the same grimy shop, testify to a needed miracle, a true wonder, a miraculous raw truth which it is one of civilization's conspiracies to suppress? And insofar as we are civilized men, men of courteous disposition and civic conscience, tolerant, sensible, and moderate, are we not members of the conspiracy, distinguishable but distinctly within it, like the few, and extra delicious, black balls within the glass sphere of the Kiwanis gum machine?

"If in this life only we have hope in Christ, we are of all men most miserable." Most miserable, for what to other men is but a hope, added to their lives as a feather to a hat, for us is the hat itself, and more than the hat, the shirt and the pants and the shoes.

We are naked, Paul tells us, if Christ be not raised—"if there be no resurrection of the dead." Yet how heavy, how heavy then and how heavier now, it is to lift the dead in cur hearts! How stony and blue they lie on the hospital dollies! How irreversible the progress of demise traced by radiographs and biopsies! And, for the living, how acceptable the death of the dead, how quickly the place seals over where they were, how slyly grateful we are for the little extra space they bequeath us! We would abhor them were they to return. One of our profoundest fears, indeed, is that the dead *will* return; the resurrection of the dead is a horror story. As a child, let me confess, I was terrified that I would pray too well, and out of the darkness Jesus would answer by walking through the door of my room, and that He would demand from me my favorite toy.

And yet, from the other standpoint, that of the infrangible *ego* who cries within us *sum* without ceasing, how much more intelligent is Paul's carnal stipulation than that neo-Platonic afterlife of spirits which survives into our age chiefly as a *mise en scène* for *New Yorker* cartoons. For we do not want to live as angels in ether; our bodies are us, us; and our craving for immortality is, as Death's great philosopher Miguel de Unamuno so correctly and devastatingly remarks, a craving not for transformation into a life beyond imagining but for our *ordinary life,* the mundane life we so driftingly and numbly live, to go on forever and forever. The only Paradise we can imagine is this Earth. The only life we desire is this one. Paul is right in his ghoulish hope, and all those who offer instead some gaseous survival of a personal essence, or one's perpetuation through children or good deeds or masterworks of art, or identification with the race of Man, or the blessedness of final and absolute rest, are tempters and betrayers of the Lord. Is not the situation in our churches indeed that from the pulpit we with our good will and wordy humanism lean out to tempt our poor sheep from those scraps of barbaric doctrine, preserved in the creed like iguanodon footprints in limestone, that alone propel them up from their pleasant beds on a Sunday morning?

Yet the resurrection of the body is impossible.

As impossible, it is fair to say, for Paul and his Corinthians as for us; for though their world had more chemical and astronomical mystery in it than ours, it also had more corpses and more observed death, more putrefying reality.

No man, unless it was Jesus, believes. We can only *profess* to believe. We stand, brethren, where we stand, in our impossible and often mischievously idle jobs, on a boundary of opposing urgencies where there is often not space enough to set one's feet—we so stand as steeples stand, as emblems; it is our station to be visible and to provide men with the opportunity to profess the impossible that makes their lives possible. The Catholic church in this at least was right; a priest is more than a man, and though the man disintegrate within his vestments, and become degraded beyond the laxest of his flock, the priest can continue to perform his functions, as a scarecrow performs his.

My brothers. Your faces, tan from the sun, fat from a month of play and liquor and tacos and tamales, look at me in my imagination, and I know your faces now, as once I knew the faces and veils of my lost suburban parish. Lightning rods for the anxieties of men, left free to roam our communities as rather laughable trouble-shooters, we naturally absorb anxiety and trouble ourselves. Perhaps we are the last salt ere the world definitively loses its savor. Or perhaps—it would be a sin for us to deny the possibility—the Parousia so imminently expected by Paul will now come, and these two millennia between will have been as the absentminded hesitation of a gracious host's hand on the way to ring for dessert, or to strike his wineglass with a knife and bring the table to attention.

In this Inbetweentimes let us take comfort at least

from the stiffness of our roles, that still stand though we crumple within them. We do not invent ourselves, and then persuade men to find room for us; rather, men invent our office, and persuade us to fill it.

Soon I must leave you, as you must leave me. We have shared a strange holiday—like nothing so much as the holiday of mourning that Confucian custom imposed upon a Mandarin who, when in the middle of his life a parent died, underwent a retreat in the mountains, far from the claims of responsibility and concubinage. And thus isolate he would compose himself for the remainder of the journey of his life. *Qui m'y a mis?* Who has set me here? The cry arises in a passage of Pascal that impressed me in the days—lost, alas, with so much else!—when I attended seminary and courted the Professor of Ethics' blossom-pale daughter. On the same page where the *Penseur* confesses his fright at the eternal silence of the infinite spaces, he confesses another fear: *je m'effraie et m'étonne de me voir ici plutôt que là, car il n'y a point de raison pourquoi ici plutôt que là, pourquoi à present plutôt que loin? Qui m'y a mis?*

Qui m'y a mis? Can the mystery, frightening and astonishing, of our existence be more clearly posed? The old mysteries erode; Henri Bergson, that graceful fellow-traveller of our rough faith, spoke of the three creaky hinges, or inexplicable gaps, in the continuum of materialism: between nothing and something, between matter and life, between life and mind. The last two have since silted in with a sludge of atomic information, and even the stark first may, eventually, reveal an anatomy: already radio telescopes have picked up a cosmic hum that apparently originates at the very rim of time.

But what could explicate and trivialize the deepest and simplest mystery, that I find myself here and not there, in the present rather than in the past or future? *Il n'y a point de raison pourquoi;* there is not a particle of reason why. So those of us who live by the irrational may moderate our shame. Who has set us here, in this vocation, at this late date, out of due time? To ask the question is to imply an answer: there is a *qui,* a Who, who has set; we have not accidentally fallen, we have been placed. As of course we already know in our marrow. God bless you. God keep you all. Amen.

[*in pencil, in the slant hand of another:*]

Yes—at last, a sermon that could be preached.

28

You spoke. You exist. The palm of my left hand tingles like that of a man with an hour to the electric chair. I did not look at my pages last evening, between golf and supper; I confess it, I surreptitiously purchased from the rear of a souvenir-and-junk shop (canvas desert bags, miniature saddles, Stetsons, high-priced foot-lengths of antique barbed wire) a little dusty green book in aid of Sunday school teachers, titled *What Boys and Girls Are Asking,* and was soaking myself in its illicit contents. So I did not see your note until this morning, settling to the typewriter that like a dull wife has grown grudgingly responsive to my touch, above the goose-dung-colored carpet where my twitching feet have worn two fluffy oblongs. The handwriting was yours as I have always imagined it—hurried yet legible, pragmatic yet a shade self-congratulatory in the formation of the capitals.

Do you truly think it a good sign, dear one, that this last sermon, lumpy with quotation and littered with pensée shavings (fact is, even were the sky a neonated 3-D billboard flashing GOD EXISTS twenty-four hours a day we would contrive ways to doubt it) and damply devoid of the neurotic and mocking fire of the others, might be preached in an actual church, with pews, blue hymnals, stained-glass betrayals and departures, and *bona fide* parishioners solidly stuffed with cotton wool? Have you been really preparing me all this time for a return to the world and not translation to a better? Is this the end of therapy, a reshouldering of ambiguity, rote performace, daily grits, hollow vows, stale gratifications, receding illusions?

Yes, is your answer, stern.

And I nod, weakly assenting. I am ready. But for one thing. One rite, one grail stands between me and a renewed reality. You, Ms. Prynne. You with your figure of perfect elegance on a large scale, your dark and abundant hair, your even darker eyes under the eyebrows as pronounced and swift in their curve as two angry strokes of unsharpened charcoal. Can I believe that the graceful extent of your neck and generous curve of your mouth ever reminded me of a turtle, albeit large and white? That I found your manner, always ladylike and dignified, once harsh, even cumbersome and bullying? That the wholly admirable briskness of your manner, fair to all and lucid to all, ever reminded me of an officious, harried, slightly-out-of-her-depth Ho-Jo hostess when the full garlanded membership of two opposed suburban garden clubs simultaneously appear for Tuesday lunch? Forgive me. I swear, I have been in love with you since the moment the jet-hum ceased in my ears. Your infallible courtesy with your redmen factotums, your beautiful glossy bun with the golden pencil stuck in it just so, your rhinestone-starred reading glasses, that so promptly yield to pilot-style shades when your duties compel you to go tap-tap-tapping along the walks of green cement that wind their crumbling way among the sand and cacti of our garden—your air of mobilized bulk, of girdled purpose that yet never disdains to pause and briskly flirt with the baby-oiled form of a disgraced cleric sunning—your delightful way of delegating and describing to your assistant Mrs. Leonora Givingly, whose crinkly timidity would in a twinkling jell to tyranny did you not so masterfully apportion out to her precise daily dopples of instruction—your slightly tossed and even tragedy-tinted sweeping way of moving along, flattening your hair with a hand tensely bent back beyond mere flatness, your sable eyes (of the type of darkness that seems hot) lifted with the heedless, faintly false, put-on bravery of the woman alone: all this has impressed me. Has pierced me. Why is there no ring on your left hand? Why have you been called to manage this desert place, this old world monastery transposed to the Columban mode of a Disneyland junket? *Qui t'y a mis?*

Once, emerging at dusk from the pool, I saw, my eyeballs chlorinated to match the sunset, you pushily passing through a double glass door from having chastened a jeaned and rebellious chambermaid, and I thought, of your ass, which had always before loomed as much beyond me as a mesa, that it was manageable. That indeed it was, for all its authoritarian majesty and apparent imperviousness, grabbable, huggable, caressable, kissable. And knew itself as such. And knew itself as such in my sunset eyes.

Why do I fancy myself silently, impassively favored? Is it from any improper acknowledgment on your part of my growing admiration, any downward smile, flirtatious blush, brazen word, any slackening at all in the taut cable of your management? No. In case these pages are surreptitiously Xeroxed and forwarded to your superiors and mine, I insist upon that exonerating negative. You have been inflexible and chaste. Wondrous strength and generosity of a woman's heart!

Yet, with the same unkillable intuition that leads me to laud the utterly *absconditus Deus,* I feel there is a place in you for me. Set aside, indeed, at your first haughty glance. When we pass in the corridor, there is a curious curvature of time-space in which our curt greeting billows and dips. When you stand by my table momently, to make your formal inquest into the edibility of the chow, I am conscious of your pelvis, presented I think deliberately at the latitude of my face, though without your stooping your pose could not be otherwise. At night, as I try, with decreasing success (the soporific effect of a strange climate long since dissipated) to sleep, I feel you somewhere on the other side of these many partitions, puzzling your way toward me, hesitating along some inbent circumference of mercy.

How charming you were, Saturday, in Sandstone, when confronted by the drunken Indian! In a suit the black of an ash-smeared stove, he halted you, there on that blinding broad sidewalk lined with bars, ranch suppliers, and vendors of postcards of canyons, as you with your fussy satellite were trying to lead back to the bus your noisy, rubicund, conspicuous pack of faulty ministers. We were too excited to be out, in a highway hamlet that looked like a city, where pickup trucks bespoke a continent of activity and agriculture, and where incongruous, faded, dryly tingling Christmas decorations festooned the hot lampposts. Our commotion had stirred this aborigine, had reached into his trance and caused him to lurch forward dustily, dressed in dirty black. It was as if you, in your dun linen dress, had suddenly grown a shadow. We halted, nonplussed, hushed. From behind me Mrs. Givingly moved toward the head of the line, clucking to herself, wound up to be officious. But with a divinely brisk wave of your hand you halted our motion, and bowed your head—smoothing back the hair on that side with a too-tense palm—to give the Indian's mumbling your ear. In truth, was not his drunkenness a groping up through firewater toward ecstasy and truth (for no other race gets drunk like this), and therefore one more of the American religious dislocations which it is your occupation to repair? He wobbled, in the unique style of drunken Indians, a graceful little stagger with a penumbra of menace to it, and pointed, all the while muttering into your ear. He was pointing at Woody; it was Woody's reactionary pride to wear the priest's bib and collar where the rest of us were in sports shirts; the Indian was offended, or interested; you, to reinforce the distinct English of your explanation, made praying hands to show a holy man, and a large circle to include us all. The Indian understood; he looked up at the sky; he laughed, and his knees suddenly bent, and you reached forward to put a hand beneath his elbow. And I, watching closely, felt with you your flicker of anticipation, your wish to move him aside so your charges could board the bus, your desire to leave this Indian—your fellow-Westerner—some dignity. Oh, I moved through you, understanding all this and more, and it came to me that love is not an e-motion, an assertive putting out, but a *trans*-motion, a compliant moving *through*.

I saw through you, with you, Ms. Prynne, in your

street ministry to that shadow caught in the sun with his cat eyes slitted by drink, and therefore presume to claim you as mine. As my end approaches, everything grows vaporous, my future and my past are the same green cloud, and only you are solid, only you have substance; I fall toward you as a meteorite toward the earth, as a comet toward the sun.

You who were kind to a drunken Indian, be kind to me, poor Wasp stung by the new work-ethic of sufficient sex, sex as the exterior sign of interior grace, as the last sanctuary for violence, conquest, and rapture, in a world as docilely crammed as an elevator ascending after lunchtime.

It occurred to me, sitting on the toilet yesterday at five (ninety swings of a golf club has a salutary loosening effect on the bowels; a second installment is produced, more contemplatively than the morning's urgent and poisoned release), that my situation with my mate Jane, with its obstinate lock of symmetry and lovingkindness, belongs to the province of works purely, and works without faith are constipation. I must cease, it seemed to me, as my happily growling guts sustained their seemingly endless process of emptying, cease regarding any lives other than my own as delivered into my care; they, and mine, are in God's care. Most of what we have is given, not acquired; a gracious acceptance is our task, and a half-conscious following-out of the veins in the circumambient lode.

This century's atrocious evils have stemmed from the previous century's glorification of the Will.

My impotence with Frankie seems now a product of overmanagement, a wish on my part to match the perfection that sat on her as lightly as a cape of feathers. If she had truly loved me, she would have maimed herself. I tried to maim her but lacked the time.

In my insomnia now, between masturbatory spurts of fantasizing about you, Ms. Prynne (your pudenda must be a gleaming heap of coal; there will be a few teasing dark hairs about your nipples), I pray; and my prayers move into the air as ripples on ripples, as a pealing of words on a kind of translucent log-road or supernatural xylophone that moves diagonally upward from me in the manner of smooth breakers, and my words are carried away in the spaces between, and are answered, not steadily, but in gusts of joy that lift me almost out of my ribs and make my early-morning hours of captivity in these gray-green walls too precious to sleep through. Next day, my golf is sloppy, and my poker scatter-brained. Even my tan is slipping away.

But it has been years since I physically felt my prayers being answered. He who is down, Bunyan tells us, need fear no fall. He who is down, says the id, is up.

I look forward respecfully to your comments.

29

Nothing. Not a word. You read me only on dull Sundays. You are repelled by my advances. You have ceased to exist. I have wasted an hour running my poor lab rat of a mind through the maze of these alternatives, and poking through the old pages looking for words from you I might have missed. Nothing. Not a word.

Today is Tuesday. Thursday I go. Think of me in the sky; think of me as a Sky-god, Uranus to your Gaea, raindrops to your desert, gospel to your despair, prattle to your silence. By what right, you ask, might I expect that you, appointed to this delicate situation because of (among other virtues, abilities, degrees in hotel and hospital management, life-saving courses at the "Y", etc.) your pronounced inseduceability, would condescend to me, a worm, a worm of the sort you process in batches?

For all I know, you are chosen for your imperviousness to clergymen, your antipathy toward them, sickly parasites as they are, consuming gasoline and heating fuel in useless missions and rituals, intruding wherever a person is gasping to death or getting married, demanding the right to say grace at the Rotary luncheon, etc. And you see the worst, the flops, a monthly gang of leprous and self-exacerbating failures.

Still, I have this mustard seed. And you have this gap in your armor. There was that air pocket when we pass in the hall. And even the rarity of encouraging helpful comments on my pages takes on a positive erotic significance. You are a gossamer ephemerid treading my edges. You are yet the end, the *intelligens entis,* of my being, insofar as I exist on paper. Give me a body. Otherwise I shall fall through space forever. Stop me.

Something keeps plucking me back from my dreams, and I stay awake for hours, hysterical as a guitar string. Last night I dreamed I was teaching my son to walk. It was not clear which son. He straightened in my arms when I picked him up, fighting to be set down. We walked on red wet tiles, his little feet between mine. Our feet were bare and wet as from the swimming pool; in a curiously adult voice, distinct though high-pitched, he remarked, in gratitude for my instruction, that I had "terrific" legs. I was so pleased I awoke. Elsewhere in the night I crossed a road with a gang of others; we stepped over one of those little guard fences of two cables on stubby posts cut on a bias; we ran down a long grassy bank dotted with daisies and butter-and-eggs; we were back home. The others ran on ahead toward the lake and Frankie waited behind with me; in a soft little gesture she unzipped her jeans and showed me her underpants. They were patterned with flowers, pale yellow and pink. It was something a child might do, for another. They were lovely. The slope of the bank and the sudden impulse of love tipped me forward, so that I awoke.

She was shy; her underpants were the nicest thing I had ever seen; did I have time to tell her so? In my dreams we have all become children, as we must, they say, to enter the kingdom of God.

The things humans do! The little creatures in the UFOs must have figured out the sex by now, and our cars, but the dreaming, and the praying, and the singing . . . How to explain music to them?

My most physical religious experience occurred in college, those first nervous years, when my poor adolescent body, just seeking to straighten and throw off its acne and stomach cramps, was cruelly loaded with the wisdom of the ages and the languages of the world. I caught colds; I had insomnia; my teeth ached; I became constitpated.* Days went by; six times a day I would sit on the hopeful porcelain oval and wait; nothing. My over-solicited anus hurt; my lower abdomen became hard as a brick; I tottered from class to class along the leafy walks in a daze of disbelief; my Christianity, never muscular, seemed a febrile useless fancy. Then, one morning, sweating over all my body, I pushed out perhaps an inch of dry compacted turd, knobby as a narwhal's tusk, and stalled; my eyes filled with tears; how could I waddle to class with this extrusion? I bent forward far as my torso would go, driven to homemade yoga in this extremity, and in my soul confessed my desperation to whatever powers there be. And a great force as if manually seized my bowels, and my body, like a magnificent animal escaped from its keeper, savagely and so swiftly the dilation of pain passed in a flash thrust out of itself a great weight of waste. It was a thrust from beyond, a release into *trans:* a true Lutherian experience, and my only. Ever since, through stress and strain, trial and tribulation, I have remained regular, as I think I bragged quite early on in these pages.

* Thinking of my constitution, or your tit. I have noticed your topload isn't as impressive as your ass, but don't let that inhibit you. Flat-chested women, between us, are some of the best. A breast is like a penis; the excitement has secondarily to do with its size; primarily with the fact that it is *there*. Existence precedes everything; *esse est deus.*

I expect my expulsion from this happy place will feel rather like that. Unless you come and love me.

I will treat you real swell, Ms. Prynne. Screwing optional, I swear it; just come and sit, tell me about your job, its difficulties, your life, its plan, the local flora, your impressions of me and the role of organized religion in the next millennium—if the chemistry is there, we'll take it all the way; otherwise, we'll have relaxed for an hour, and been kind to one another. No hassle, really. I just feel we have a potential, there's something between us it would be a sin not to let happen. Have I been a bad guest? Have I complained about the food, tried to smuggle postcards out, attempted to bugger the serving boys, held private Masses in my room, refused to play card games because the Devil speaks in pips, faked fragile health and bribed the doctor to sign my release, pulled sacerdotal rank on you, gone crazy and smashed my typewriter, like some we know? No. I've been a fun boy, faithful to my vows of obedience, full of the right camp spirit, willing to learn, anxious under all my impudence to return to the world as a good exemplar if not a good *exemplum*. I want my merit badge. You, Ms., pynne it on me. At night if you wish, but I'm fresher and more phallic in the morning. Incline unto me, and hear my cry.

I love you because (a) you are there (b) you run this haven ably (c) you never complain (d) you seem to be alone (e) you read what I write.

You love me because (a) I am here (b) I need you.

Oh, never mind. Suddenly it is noon, and the universe has shrunk for me to a single circle of white suds, the cool galactic foam that tops a Daiquiri.

30

Then don't come, you bitch. You sashaying cunt. I hardly slept a dream's worth, for listening for your step, your fingers on the latch, the rustle of your silk, the little tearful twinned *suck* as you remove the contact lenses it is your vanity to wear when you go out with one of your dreadful square-state "dates." You didn't know I knew that about you, did you? Old Tom Marshfield, he has his spies, to paraphrase Lear.

Seriously. Good-bye. I can write hardly a page today, I have said everything I can think of at least twice concerning my lamentable case, and have wasted the morning in packing and listening for you. Packing, I suppose, on the remote chance, the odds Pascalian, that you will relent and come to me tomorrow morning. The plane isn't until two, there would be time. Time to cheat time.

I am delirious with poor sleeping. It will be a relief to crawl in beside Jane's stony slumber and become a stone myself. Here lieth Thomas and his mate Jane, petrified in the Lord's service, left here as a monument and admonition to passersby.

What else can I imagine about the future? Froggy-eyed Ned sits in the middle of my old lily pad; I expect I will be banished to a remote village parish, where once every Midsummer's Eve the villagers will bring to me a virgin lass as to a Minotaur, and I in turn will perform, every vernal equinox, some miracle, involving a sprinkle of my own blood, to keep the crops coming and their lives innocently merry. So be it. I submit.

The worst thing was cleaning (with a fork snitched from your incandescent dining room with the tall drawn vanilla curtains) all the dirt from the cleats of my golf shoes, so my summer clothes (so spiffily purged and pressed at the Peyote Dry Cleaners) wouldn't be sullied while shivering in the belly of the great aluminum bird. I have used up eleven razor blades and two tubes of toothpaste in this heaping measure of a month's time. In the land of my parish, the shortest day of the year is approaching, and Somebody's birthday, I think, the little fellow who never manages to blow out all of the candles.

Eschatological satisfaction of leaving things behind—two pairs of worn socks, one short-sleeved sports shirt whose seam gave out on an overswung 3-iron, one bottle of Coppertone, bone-dry. Outer darkness. The Superworld's Disposall. Our tenderized consciences wince, but there may be a mercy in it.

Do I want to take *What Boys and Girls Are Asking* back with me? I open it randomly and read,

> In attempting to answer the question, "What can we discover concerning the existence and the nature of God from the life around us?" Doctor Gilkey used for an illustration the example of a shipwrecked sailor who finds a deserted cabin on an island.

> Another question which often perplexes boys and girls was expressed by one boy in this way: "Why did God let Jesus die on the cross?" If a leader has a Christian philosophy of his own with regard to the death of Christ he may lead boys and girls into a helpful consideration of this.

> The bright morning sun beat down on the little Chinese village. For weeks the people had looked hopefully toward the sky for signs of rain. Rain could still save the crops. But no rain fell, and the rice fields withered in the scorching heat.
>
> It was with a heavy heart that the Rev. Mr. Lu-Cheng-sun entered the tiny church building.

I guess I must take it. As a souvenir.

The immanence of departure renders this bland room as strange as when I entered it. I leave no trace, no scar. Did I dream this? Meister Eckhardt, if I remember, talks of divinity as "the simple ground, the quiet desert" and of a process, so God can be born in the soul, of *entwerden,* the opposite of becoming, travelling away from oneself. The day after tomorrow, my month may seem a metaphor, a pause briefer than that rest of Alicia's I so reprehensibly interrupted.

Last night after poker I went out under the dome of desert stars and was afraid, not afraid, afraid to be born again.

Even so, come.

31

The suitcases stand in parade formation by the closet door, their zipped zippers and snapped snaps as disapproving as spinsters' mouths. I am terrified. Up in the air. My life here, like my life from birth, seems all loose ends. Is there really no more sense than this? Flight has already entered my stomach and set it to trembling. I cannot cope. I cannot

Bless you.

What a surprise. Your knock wasn't the knock of doom after all. What remains, at this moment, a moment of this my last hour, was the brave way in which you undressed without comment, disclosing with not the flicker of a plea that you were, not fat, but thick, certainly thick, so that my startled arms, embracing, felt to be encircling the trunk of a solid but warm tree. And the tranquillity of you upon your back! Permitting your breasts to be molded again and again—amazing breasts, so firm they seemed small, the nipples erect upon little mounds of further erectile tissue, so that a cupola upon a dome was evoked, an ascent in several stages, an architectural successiveness. Difficult, from your profile, to guess your pleasure. You seemed lost in thought, only your hand speaking to me, lightly drawing my penis up into its ideal shape, so it could once again lose its ache in the almost—nay, veritably—alarmingly liquid volume of the passage to your womb. The entire process indolent, chronic, tranquil. How many times? I did lose count. I feel drained, light; I have a fever, a light headache. Was I worthy? You have brought me to an edge, a slippery edge. And nothing left for me to do, dear Ideal Reader, but slip and topple off, gratefully.

What is it, this human contact, this blank-browed thing we do for one another? There was a moment, when I entered you, and was big, and you were already wet, when you could not have seen yourself, when your eyes were all for another, looking up into mine, with an expression without a name, of entry and alarm, and of salutation. I pray my own face, a stranger to me, saluted in turn.

Other Novels by John Updike

THE POORHOUSE FAIR R543 60¢

A novel about a fair held in the 1970's, in which the poorhouse is the setting and the theme is a struggle for the soul of America.

RABBIT, RUN P2150 $1.25

A frank treatment of a former high school athlete, Harry "Rabbit" Angstrom, and his failure to cope with the adult world.

THE CENTAUR P2115 $1.25

The myth of Chiron, the noblest and wisest of the Centaurs, retold in a contemporary setting.

OF THE FARM M476 95¢

A delicate psychological study of a man's relationship to his mother, his wife, and his stepson.

COUPLES Q2167 $1.50

A powerful novel of life in an authentically decadent community.

RABBIT REDUX Q1753 $1.50

In this sequel to *Rabbit, Run*, Harry Angstrom, suffering through a failed marriage, is caught in a clash of values between conservative Middle America and the new counterculture.

FAWCETT

Wherever Paperbacks Are Sold

If your bookdealer is sold out, send cover price plus 35¢ each for postage and handling to Mail Order Department, Fawcett Publications, Inc., P.O. Box 1014, Greenwich, Connecticut 06830. Please order by number and title. Catalog available on request.